A Place That Used to Be

More Books by Brittni Brinn

The Patch Project

More Books by Adventure Worlds Press

The Synthetic Albatross Series

The Thinking Machine
The Neon Heart
Broadcast Wasteland

No Light Tomorrow

The Space Between Houses

A Place That Used to Be

Brittni Brinn

A Place That Used to Be
brittnibrinn.com

First Printing, June 2020

This is a work of fiction. Names, characters, places, and incidences are products of the author's imagination or are used fictionally and are not construed as real. Any resemblance to actual events, locations, organizations, or persons, living or dead, is entirely coincidental.

Printed in Canada.

Published by
Adventure Worlds Press
Windsor Ontario

ISBN 978-0-9949803-7-3 (Paperback)

Edited by Amilcar John Nogueira
Layout by Ben Van Dongen
Cover design by Christian Laforet
Author photo by Sarah Kivell

For Liam,
I promised your parents that I would
dedicate my next book to their unborn child
and then you were born.

Table of Contents

Book One

Chapter 1
Worth Keeping

Jeff didn't expect to find much. The rusted carcass of a tractor, or wood from a broken-down fence, maybe. But the green had caught his eye, a scattering of grass and clover at first, then a rolling field, a double-crested hill rising from its centre. Worth a look, at least.

According to the plastic speedometer affixed to his handlebars, he was going about 10 km/hr. Not bad for rough terrain. The air smelled fresh and clean as he cut through; tall stalks of alfalfa and grass brushed past his knees. He pushed the pedals faster, keeping an eye out for abandoned farm equipment or wild animals. For other Grafters, most of all.

It had been days since the last patch: an abandoned truck, the tires missing, most of the engine stripped. Luckily, Grafters didn't always know what was worth keeping. He'd got some wires out of the dash, and the cigarette lighter from under the gaping hole where the tape deck used to be. He'd found a flat of water bottles in a hideaway panel under the floor mat, and a case of rations wedged behind the back seat, including a covered pan of popcorn kernels, campfire-ready.

Jeff approached the foot of the double hill and clamped the brakes shut in his travel-sore hands. Hopping down from his bike seat, he set the kickstand and unclipped his helmet, leaving the straps to hang down on either side of his face. He scratched at his thick dark beard. Before anything else, he checked the hitch connecting the covered trailer to his bike. Secure as he could hope for.

Reaching for the water bottle at his waist, Jeff surveyed the green. The field must've spread from a smaller patch; he pictured it creeping outwards into the wasteland. A couple metres to his left was an old fence post, rusted barbed wire flaring from either side. Empty cans with serrated tops and a cracked shovel head littered the ground around it.

Jeff squinted at the clear grey sky. Using the broken shovel head, he cleared a shallow pit in a bare patch of soil. He took an axe from his bike trailer and felled the fence post, cutting through the weathered wood in two hits, the barbed wire crumpling as he threw the whole post into the pit. He gathered some loose clumps of grass, light yellow and dead, from the field.

Flint to knife blade. Ear to the ground. Using his lungs as bellows, pushing air through his cheeks. A catching glow, creeping up the dry stalks to find footing in the wood. Spurts of flame.

Stars started to show. Sitting with his back to the double hill, Jeff held the wire handle suspending the covered aluminum pan over the low burn. It slowly started to expand and snap with sound, a tapping from the inside, kernels getting kinetic. He shook the pan, let it rest another moment over the embers and then set it next to him in the dirt. He took a sip from his water bottle. The silver ring on his pinky reflected the dying firelight.

When the pan was cool enough, he peeled back the billow of silver foil. The first piece of popcorn was salt and crunch with a warm heart. Not burnt, he was happy to note. Jeff took another kernel from the pan. He chewed it slowly as he scanned the darkened landscape and looked up at the stars.

A light breeze disturbed the field, waving dim shadows and rustling alfalfa stalks against each other. Jeff covered the remaining half of the popcorn. There were cracks of fire left in the pit, pulsing dimly in the black. Jeff placed the leftovers, the axe, and the shovel head in the back of the bike trailer; he returned to his place by the campfire with a sleeping bag and a flashlight.

Something stopped him as he settled in. Something going against the flow of the breeze, rippling the alfalfa at the wrong moment. Jeff quickly pinpointed the source: a figure coming towards him, making no effort to quiet their steps. Jeff pointed the flashlight at the figure and toggled the thick plastic button.

"Jesus," the stranger said, lifting a hand to shield his face from the sudden light.

Jeff was already on his feet, guarding his bike with his body.

"I saw your fire." The stranger lowered his hand. "It's been ages since anyone's come this way."

"You live around here?"

"Just around the corner." A note of humor tinged the stranger's voice.

Jeff kept the circle of light on the stranger's face. "Don't believe you." Jeff thought about rushing the stranger but didn't want the unpleasant surprise of a knife in the stomach or a bullet in the eye. So, he waited.

The stranger held out a hand, offering something. "I thought you might be hungry." He dipped out of the beam, placing the something on the ground. Whistling, he walked off into the field. An old song, something Jeff recognized from the radio, years ago.

Jeff followed him with the flashlight, as far as it would go. He flicked the light down to where the stranger had placed the something. It looked like a small cardboard box.

Could be a trick. Could be explosive, or poisoned, be full of broken glass.

But it didn't smell right. It was warm, with something like Christmas in it.

Crouching down, Jeff lifted the flaps of the shallow cardboard box. Stark in the harsh beam of his flashlight sat a sliced loaf of homemade gingerbread.

Brittni Brinn

Chapter 2
Light Bringer

Rhonda stepped onto the sun-warmed stair and let the weighted metal door swing shut behind her. Her hand settled on the back of a stone lion that sat attentive on the bannister. She took in the familiar landscape: a short concrete pathway joined the bottom step to a segment of cracked asphalt cutting through the overgrown front lawn. The segment abruptly ended where the wasteland began, the flat tan sea that surrounded the school she called home.

She headed down the pathway, her flip flops slapping against the concrete. Turning onto the lawn, she glanced back; the brick facade of the school building was starting to develop a lattice of shadows in the evening light.

Rhonda found Milo relaxing on a square of mown grass a ways into the otherwise unkempt lawn. The yellow solar generator sat next to him.

"How's the battery?" she asked.

"As good as it's gonna get, day's almost over." Milo unplugged the charger from the generator, handing it to her. A light on the grey battery inside blinked green and then faded as the charger lost power. "Should last you a few hours."

"Thanks, I'll need it."

"What you working on?"

"Some documentary footage." Rhonda pocketed the charger

and battery. "I'll show you when I'm done, as usual."

"Less butter on the popcorn this time." Milo had a quiet smile, no teeth; the corners of his mouth pushed up his cheeks, emphasizing the wrinkles.

"You got it."

Rhonda reached for the generator.

"I'll take care of that," Milo said as he settled back onto the short grass.

"You sure?"

"You saying I can't handle it?"

Rhonda laughed, once. "Not at all, old man."

"'Night, Rhonda."

"'Night."

She headed back to the school, and climbed the three concrete steps, resting a hand on the stone lion's face as she passed. Stooping so that the lanyard around her neck would have enough slack, she fit her key into the handle, unlocked the door, and went in.

The front door banged shut, sending echoes into the tiled hallway. A row of lockers gaped open on either side; she passed between them and turned right, stopping to unlock the red door with a thin rectangle of meshed window.

Heavy blinds hung in grey swaths over three tall windows behind the counter. A small picture window, set up near the ceiling, was the only light bringer. It used to have a blind over it as well, but she'd pulled it down early on to use as a bed mat. She set the charged battery on the counter, which was bare otherwise. The washed shirt she'd laid across the chair that morning was crisp around the edges. Everything was as it should be.

You couldn't be too careful, though. Grafters were getting bolder. Travelers crossed the wasteland in groups now, some with protection—guns were rare, but were around. She thought back to the trade caravan that had come through a week before: the man with the shotgun on the back of the wagon, glaring at the stub of road, glaring at them. Even Milo, usually at ease with

8

the traders who came through, kept away from him. In the end, they'd gotten butter for a couple of minor repairs to the traders' wagon, and the man with the shotgun had remained aloof. Of course, none of the traders knew about the stockpile of filming equipment Rhonda had hidden in the wall.

She leaned down under the small window, taking time to settle to her knees. Her stomach was beginning to thicken again. She and Milo were in what they called "the good times": the garden out back was heavy with vegetables and caravans stopped by once a month or so, bringing full cans and jars and day-old eggs. Rhonda had always been on what her mother called "the fatter side." "Too much sitting in front of that damned computer," she'd say, "Needs an active man. Someone to go to the gym with." Her mom had been no magazine model either, but Rhonda figured that was the kind of thing older women liked to say to young people. Live through them, somehow.

Rhonda pushed down the memory and ran her hand over the rippled texture of the wall. The bottom half was lined with thin wooden slats, maybe to dampen sound, or to give a rustic '70s flair to the room. Rhonda found the tab of clear packing tape and pulled gently. A section of the wall hinged outward to reveal a small cache. It had been her idea to hide her equipment here and Milo had built it. He had a cache of his own in the janitor closet, though Rhonda was polite enough not to ask where it was.

"Goddammit," she swore under her breath, remembering that her battery was still on the counter. The high window was grey velvet, the daylight fading. She crawled to the other side of the room, grabbed the battery and headed back to the open space in the wall. A quick glance to the blank window assured her that no one was watching. It wouldn't take much for someone to piece together that she had a hiding spot and where it was. She tucked the battery into her camera bag and replaced the wall panel, a little reluctantly. She wanted to start on her documentary today, but there wasn't enough light left to film by.

She did her rounds of the room. Checking the deadbolt and

handle lock on the door, making sure each of the windows behind the blinds was still in one piece. She folded the dry shirt and placed it in one of the drawers under the counter. She took off her pants and draped them over the chair back and then kicked her flip flops underneath the seat.

Laying on the old blind, she readjusted the bag of soundproofing foam under her head. She reached for the crocheted blanket she'd gotten in exchange for a computer keyboard. The nights were getting cooler. Soon she'd be sleeping in her fitted wool jacket, waking up to the sight of her breath hovering overhead.

Silence curled around her. It was full night now, the chair across the room nothing more than a dim blob. The picture window framed a couple of pinhole stars. Rhonda took deep breaths, trying to keep her mind on what she would film tomorrow and not on the sound of broken glass that threatened to fill the room at any moment.

Nothing protected her here. Windows were weak. The Grafters would have guns. It would take them a moment to find her, not expecting anyone to be inside. They would threaten her. She wouldn't tell them anything. They would tear through her drawers, wrench open the closet. They would go over the walls with flashlights. One would stand guard over her, the muzzle of a shotgun pressing down on her chest. The gleam of the packing tape would give it away. They would tear open her cache, rip her guts out.

Go to sleep, she commanded herself—her heartbeat pounded in her ears, her mouth was dry—

Milo's just down the hall, she tried next, he'll hear the breaking glass and rush in with the axe—but the Grafters would kill him too.

Once she was asleep, nothing could touch her—but there was a wall between her and the dreamworld and there was no door. Rhonda lay on her mat, paralyzed with fear.

She forced her thoughts away from images of blood and breaking windows and thought instead of her first boyfriend,

Matthew J. He had clever eyes and gentle hands. She imagined him as he would be now: taller than her, his glossy black hair brushing his shoulders. Still in love with her.

"Kiss me," she said, slipping his hand down the front of her jeans.

He stayed for a while, and then was gone. She lay alone under the blanket, eyes closed, her legs open. Then in reverse. Legs sliding closed, eyes flickering open.

Stars caught in the high window like fireflies. The chair a rounded tombstone.

It was silent without him. It was dark. There were windows. There were guns.

Help, her mind whispered as she fell asleep. Help... help... help...

Brittni Brinn

Chapter 3
Vehicle of Choice

The open sleeping bag slid from Jeff's shoulders as he shook himself fully awake. He'd spent the night sitting with his back to the hill, watching the field. Should've moved on, he thought to himself for the hundredth time, even though the stranger hadn't returned. The box of gingerbread sat next to him, the cardboard flaps closed to keep in the smell.

Jeff rolled his aching shoulders and got to his feet. Stumbling a little as he made the short trip to the bike trailer, he picked up the leftover popcorn, threw his empty water bottle into the back and dug a full one out from under his axe. Dropping breakfast on his sleeping bag as he passed, he went a little into the alfalfa and relieved himself.

The sun, sitting halfway up on the horizon, resembled a burning red contact lens. Around Jeff it was a cool grey. He settled next to the ash-filled fire pit, still smoking from the night before. Pulling the sleeping bag around his midsection, he peeled the silver cover from the rest of the popcorn. The crunch was still there, but it was stale, the butter flavor congealed in the crevices. He chewed his way through as much as he could.

The box next to him—one of those fold up take-out containers, somewhere between pink and purple—reminded him of the bakery down the street, when the city was still there. A place he'd buy croissants on the way to class. A place he'd meet dates for coffee.

The memory strong on his tongue, Jeff used his pinky to flip open one of the thin cardboard flaps. The bread was clearly homemade, rough slices shaped more like amoebas than uniform squares. He lifted the box in one hand, used the other to waft the smell towards him as if in chemistry class. You never wanted to smell a chemical straight on, he remembered. Could burn. Fumes could kill. But he couldn't smell anything besides hunger and sugar warmed over.

"I'm afraid I'm not much of a baker."

The stranger's voice shot through him. The edge of the box crumpled in Jeff's grip. This is it, he thought. Should've moved on.

The stranger sat down across from him. Flashing an immaculate set of teeth, he reached over and took one of the slices from Jeff's frozen hands. Jeff followed the gingerbread as the stranger took a bite.

"I thought about leaving you alone," he said after swallowing, "but you were positively agonizing over it, you know that? I couldn't even see your face, and I could tell."

Jeff stared at the stranger for a moment. Then he crammed a piece of bread into his mouth.

The stranger laughed. "That's more like it!"

They finished off the gingerbread together. Jeff sat back, studying the stranger. He was thin, not gaunt, with pale skin, hazel eyes, and honey brown hair shaved along one side. His clothes were old, but neat and form-fit. He wasn't a Grafter. He was too relaxed, too soft.

"So, I'm Caden. Nice to meet you." The stranger held out a hand. Jeff shook it, feeling the lightness against his own rough palm.

"Jeff."

Caden grinned. "I see you're an engineer. Or are pinky rings a fad among Grafters these days?"

"Mechanical engineer."

"And a bike is your vehicle of choice?"

"Haven't found anything better. Bikes don't need gas. They're easier to fix. Lightweight, easier to hide."

"Smart." Caden paused, flicking his eyes up past Jeff.

Jeff turned to follow his glance, expecting to see a far-off caravan or a lone Grafter stalking towards them, but the domes behind him were clean, short grass gleaming in the morning sun.

Caden folded up the empty cardboard box. "I assume you're good at fixing things."

"Depends. What are we talking?"

"I'm not sure. Maybe it can't be fixed."

Jeff stood up and brushed the crumbs from his beard and his shirt. "You gave me a meal. Only fair I try to help you out. Let's take a look."

"I appreciate it." Caden placed a light hand on his arm. "Follow me."

Brittni Brinn

Chapter 4
Carrot

Milo tipped the bucket, draining his shaving water around the roots of the tomatoes. Thankfully, plants didn't mind hair, and soap was okay by them too. It was dark out, and quiet, the spicy fragrance of tomato leaves filling his head. An herbal smell, sharp around the edges. He could almost taste a BLT, with a generous layer of mayonnaise. A few years ago, the thought would have depressed him. Mayo, cheese, bacon, even bread, they were impossible. Sucked up with the rest of the world into oblivion.

But now, traders were starting to carry things like homemade butter sealed in jars and the occasional hunk of dry bread. People out there were making things, helping each other make them. Someone had to have an oven to cook things in, after all, and someone else had to have a cow or goat to get milk from. Someone had to find or make flour. Someone had to know the recipe. So, maybe mayo wasn't so far off. They'd made it before, they could make it again.

Milo straightened slowly, taking a moment to listen. Nothing strange in the silence. No rabbits scratching at the high wooden fence that kept them and other garden thieves at bay. He felt for the button on the side of his wristwatch; the silver face glowed green, the hands at 4:11 a.m., the second hand ticking steadily along. The battery in his watch had lasted much longer than expected, but it was only a matter of time.

He stepped over the pumpkin patch and reached the rain barrel, dipping the bucket through the disc of water inside it, his fingers curling at the sudden chill waiting underneath. He emptied one bucket's worth over the garden and went back for another. The lettuce and carrots would need some extra tonight. He was hoping for a harvest the next afternoon, to thin them out, make room for the growing generation coming in. For now, he uprooted a small carrot and secured it in one of his bulky vest pockets for later.

The burning in his side started up again, cutting deep. Milo rested his back against the brick wall of the school, pressing on the pain with his palm. He found a couple of stars. Casting curious glances over the top of the fence like friendly neighbours. Hello, Cassiopeia. Evening, Orion. Nods all around.

The pain passed. "Indigestion," he hoped aloud. He filled another bucket and carried it out of the garden, securing the gate behind him.

He didn't bother with his flashlight. Out here, it could attract the wrong kind of attention. Besides, he knew the lawn, the school building on his right looming black with the eggshell gleam of the moon caught in its windows. He always marveled at how bright the moon was. Stripped of competition, it held court on the front lawn, that ghostly lady in the sky. Myths hung haloed around her, and every star dimmed a little in comparison.

Milo made his way up the concrete stairs, one arm curled around the bucket, the other steady on the stone banister. He paused. A dull hum rumbled in the distance. Milo set the bucket on the top step. The humming grew louder, grinding in his ears.

Thinking quickly, he jogged down the front walkway and veered to the left. He tucked himself into the outhouse, a displaced bathroom cubicle that he and Rhonda had carried out of the school and set up on the lawn. The humming was almost on top of him now. He flipped the door open and strolled along the asphalt in the direction of the school, pretending not to notice the motorcycle that was slowing down next to him.

"Hey!" the Grafter yelled. He flicked on his headlight, drowning out the moonlight, bringing the school to stark attention. "Old man!"

Milo started as if surprised and stopped walking. "Hello?" he said in a feeble voice. He turned slowly to face the man on the bike.

"Yeah you!" The Grafter jumped down and strode towards him. "Don't move."

Milo nodded absently.

The Grafter studied him for a moment. "You live here?"

"Yes, yes. I live here."

"Anyone else?"

Milo slowly shook his head. "It's so lonely... So lonely." He added a wavering sigh, for effect.

Narrowing his eyes, the Grafter looked up at the truncated school building. "I bet you have quite the stash in there."

"Just enough for an old man like me. Not much left." Milo cast his eyes down. "If it wasn't for the last trade caravan, I—"

"Trade caravan?"

"Yes. They came through a couple days ago. All kinds of food, supplies. They had clothes, and eggs."

The Grafter grabbed Milo's throat. "Are you lying to me?"

"No," he croaked out, "look, look." Milo pointed to his pocket. The Grafter snapped it open, rifled through it more roughly than necessary.

The Grafter let Milo go, staring at the carrot in his hand. "Damn."

Milo rubbed his neck and let out a small cough. "I... I repaired one of their wheels. With the one rusted wrench I have left, but... it worked well enough... They gave me a carrot and a jar of butter as thanks. The butter was delicious. The carrot... I was saving the carrot."

"Which way did they go?" The Grafter was fixated on the carrot, as if he was afraid it would bite him if he looked away.

Keeping a hand over his throat, Milo pointed weakly to his left, over the Grafter's motorcycle, back into the wasteland.

"You'd better not be lying to me."

"Could… could I have my carrot back… please… it's all I have—"

The Grafter lunged at Milo. Milo flinched, his hands raising to ward off the attack.

Laughing, the Grafter shoved Milo to the ground. He was still laughing as he started up his motorcycle and turned off his headlight. Milo stayed frozen, the asphalt cool against his cheek, until the roaring of the Grafter's engine faded entirely away.

Milo straightened up, thankful for the night silence around him. He steadied his breathing and let go of the heightened awareness that came along with the use of his ability. There was no further need to convince anyone of anything. The Grafter was gone.

He thought of the Grafter's amazement at the carrot and laughed. "Poor sap." He felt a small twinge of guilt. The caravan had a gun. If he caught up, the Grafter on the motorcycle wouldn't get far unless he was willing to trade fair. "Up to him," Milo reminded himself. For now, at least, he and Rhonda were safe.

Picking the bucket off the top step, Milo took a moment to appreciate the night air. The moon inclined towards the horizon and a slight grey diffused up from the east. He still had a few things to do before heading to bed. He unlocked the front door, tucked his key ring into the breast pocket of his vest, and went inside.

Chapter 5
Inside

"No need to worry about that."

Jeff looked up from his bike, his grip tightening around the handlebars. "I'm not leaving it here."

"You'll be able to keep an eye on it, it's not far."

Jeff reset the kickstand. "Just around the corner?"

Caden's smile grew. He waved and walked around the back of the double hill. Jeff followed, trying to ignore his twisting insides, screaming at him to run back for his bike. Everything he owned was in the trailer. Without it, he'd be stuck with no supplies and no way to cross the wasteland. It would take him days to walk to the nearest settlement.

"Man, you're wound tight. Relax. It's just up here."

"Up…?"

Caden scaled one of the hills. Once he reached the crest, he did a brief look around. Scanning for Grafters, Jeff assumed. Caden crouched, opening a hatch of turf, and jumped down inside of the hill.

"Incredible," Jeff breathed, hurrying to follow Caden. He lived *inside*? How'd he hollow out a hideout like that? Why have a top entry instead of a door? He'd have had to put up supports to prevent collapse. And there would have to be ventilation of some kind. It seemed impossible. What could Caden have in there? What did he want help fixing?

"Come on down!" Caden called through the opening.

Jeff dropped into the interior, finding himself in a dimly-lit dome. "You have to tell me how—" Jeff stopped short. His vision adjusted, clarifying the edges. "Holy shit."

Jeff and Caden were standing comfortably inside what looked like a single-room apartment. A small kitchenette on the left, something that looked like a treadmill on the right. A fold-out single bed yawned open from the back wall. A dim glow emanated from the ceiling. But the real impossibility was right in front of them: a wall of screens. All off except for one. A blue circle hanging in the middle of it.

Caden rested his hand on the back of the chair in front of the screens. "I was pretty surprised, too. I thought aliens, government experiments. But my curiosity got the better of me. It's one of my flaws. Being too curious." He swiveled the chair, an invitation. His hazel eyes were fixed on Jeff.

Jeff accepted. The chair was padded and comfortable, its solid base built into the floor; it spun easily with him as he turned to face the glowing screen. There was no control board, no physical inputs or buttons. Just the chair and the wall of screens, all within his reach. Jeff raised a finger and tapped the blue circle. Two more screens switched on, one showing four symbols, the other a mosaic of outside views. His bike sat undisturbed in the top right quadrant.

He tried tapping on a blank screen, but nothing happened. "This is what you want me to fix?"

"It's not broken, per se. I just have no idea how it works."

"Have you tried turning it off and on again?"

Caden smirked at the joke. "It's all yours."

Jeff drew into himself, not wanting to believe it.

"You can stay here. Try to crack the code, if you want."

Jeff scanned the interior. The kitchenette promised food. A fold-out bed, he hadn't slept in a real bed in months.

"Why?" he searched Caden's expression, "I could strip the place and disappear."

"You could." Caden stared him down. "But I don't think you

will. Call it intuition."

Something clicked in Jeff's head. "Can you...read my mind? Is that what the Event did to you?"

A cascade of laughter. "You believe those mutant stories going around?"

"Some people say—"

"Don't worry. I'm not psychic or anything, believe me. Make yourself at home. You can bring your bike in here if you want."

Jeff stood up from the chair, a strange mixture of joy and disbelief mingling in his stomach.

"I'm right next door if you need me."

The double hill. "There's two of them."

Caden nodded. "I'm sure you'll have a lot of questions about how the kitchen works. I'll drop by this evening, if that's okay." He stretched his long arms over his head and yawned. "I was up all night."

Jeff shook his head. "You were watching me."

"I was watching out *for* you. Grafters don't come often, but a patch of green is usually enough to draw some interest."

"Thanks."

"Don't mention it. Besides, it's nice to have a conversation with someone other than myself." Caden pulled a stepladder from the wall. "I've missed that." He climbed out of the dome, closing the hatch behind him.

The walls brightened slowly. Jeff sat on the bed, staring at the puzzle of screens ahead of him. The image of his bike and trailer was so small, so unfamiliar. Should bring them in, he thought. But he couldn't move. He didn't want to break the moment, the ecstatic sensation of being inside of a place that shouldn't exist.

Brittni Brinn

Chapter 6
Figure

Rhonda had just tucked her camera into her bag when she noticed a smudge on the wasteland. A dim blob the size of her thumb. It took her a moment to realize that the growing smudge was not a smudge at all, but a person. Someone was walking towards the school.

A knot started to twist up her stomach. Rhonda ignored it and squinted at the figure. It was hard to tell anything about them at this distance. Grey sweater with the hood up, black cargo pants. Definitely wearing a backpack.

Rhonda glanced back at the school. The windows in the brick wall were all covered. Only a corner of the garden was visible, just a broken-down old fence, no greenery peeking through. Nothing immediately attractive to a Grafter. But she knew that wouldn't stop them from trying to get in. She could try to find Milo, but then she'd give away their entry point to the stranger, who was steadily getting closer.

Should she pretend to be a Grafter? That she just stumbled on the place herself? She'd done it before, to a young guy with his front teeth missing, before Milo "discovered" them trying to get in the front door and chased them off with an axe. Just to be safe, she'd walked half a day before turning back to find Milo sitting on the front steps skinning a rabbit. The other Grafter stayed away. Found something better, maybe. Or starved to death out in the wasteland.

The figure reached the road and continued walking. Rhonda could make out their hiking boots, the hint of a nose and chin under the curve of the hood. Deciding bold was better, she approached the figure, hands in the pockets of her jeans. She realized that she only had a satchel with her and was wearing a pair of lime green flip-flops, not very travel-worthy for a Grafter, but she could come up with something if pressed.

The figure caught sight of her and stopped. They were waiting for her approach, sizing her up.

"I got here first!" Rhonda yelled. "Finders keepers!"

The figure didn't respond right away. They took their time drawing back their hood. "Does Milo live here?" they called.

Rhonda was taken aback by a few things. Firstly, the figure was a young woman, and it was a rare thing for a woman to be travelling alone. Second, the woman knew about Milo. And third, half of her face was scarred, a shock of dead white hair clouding her forehead.

"Who?" Rhonda pulled herself together. She had to keep up the act, until she was sure.

"Milo," the woman replied. "I'm here to see him."

"Oh." It seemed pointless to say anything else. The woman looked at her steadily, her irises dark brown, almost black. Should she invite the woman inside? Should she ask her to wait?

Seeming to understand Rhonda's hesitation, the woman crouched down on the asphalt, facing away from the school wing. She settled to the ground, shuffling off her pack. "I won't look." The back of her hair was a few shades lighter than her eyes, cut ragged just shy of her shoulders. Her hands rested on her knees.

Rhonda ran to the front door, but before she could take out her key, Milo appeared from the other side of the school building.

"What's wrong?" he asked as she reached him, and immediately scanned the edge of the lawn.

Rhonda pointed behind her, gathering her breath.

"There's... she knows your name... wants to talk to you."

Milo's face folded into a frown, but quickly smoothed itself. "Better not keep her waiting, then." He walked towards the small figure sitting on the road.

The woman sensed their approach and rose slowly. She turned to face them with her hands out, as if to show they were empty. Like before, she waited. Studied them.

Milo stopped a few feet away from the woman. No signs of recognition passed between them. "Good afternoon," Milo said.

"You're Milo."

"Yes, though I'm not sure to what I owe the pleasure." He extended a hand.

The woman gripped it briefly without breaking eye contact. "I'm the doctor."

"Ah," Milo said, casting a quick look at Rhonda. "This is my, uh, daughter, Rhonda."

"You can call me Pinot." The woman said with a slight lifting of her mouth, her eyelids.

"A doctor?" Rhonda looked to Milo, the knot returning to her stomach.

Milo nodded. "I asked for her to come."

"Why?"

Milo pointed over to Pinot, who had picked up her bag. "Let's get our guest settled before we get into all of that."

"Is something wrong?"

"Wrong?" he cleared his throat. "'Course not."

Rhonda didn't follow them up the stairs. She heard the door thump closed behind them. Staring out past the edge of the lawn, she stood in the tall grass, twisting broken-off strands between her fingers. Her lungs burned, her heart was tightening, like a balloon trying to expand inside of a glass bottle. She tried to picture herself sitting in a canoe in the middle of a calm lake, or on a bench in a quiet park. But there were storm clouds gathering; Milo was sitting next to her on the bench—suddenly leaning forwards, clutching at his chest, or his stomach, his head—

"Rhonda?"

She started, crushing the grass in her hands. Pinot stood in front of her, with that same open-handed gesture. Meaning no harm.

"You're upset he didn't tell you. I see this a lot," she stepped closer to Rhonda, "People don't want their families to worry. They want to know what's wrong before they say anything."

"Is Milo… is he really sick?"

Pinot lowered her hands. "I don't know yet. It'll take a day or two for me to be sure."

"Sure of what?"

"If there's something serious." Pinot motioned for Rhonda to follow her back into the school. "He has some abdominal pain. I can observe the symptoms, but I can't do much more than that." She started up the stone steps, then turned back. "You're not really his daughter, are you?"

Rhonda hesitated a moment, then shook her head.

"You never know who you can trust out here. Good to stick with the people you know."

"We've been here since the beginning."

"You're as good as each other's family, then. I'll do what I can."

Milo opened the front door. He avoided Rhonda, speaking instead to Pinot. "There's a room for you across the hall. Something to eat? It must've been quite the trek to get here."

"Thanks," Pinot said. "It's been a long road."

Chapter 7
Dome Sweet Dome

There were four white symbols, a dense collection of dashes and ragged dots, each encased in a circle. Tapping on them did nothing. Jeff tried dragging one across the screen. It remained fixed. He tried pressing them in different orders. He swiped left—the symbols didn't move.

"Any luck?" Caden asked from the kitchenette. He was mixing powder with filtered water from a tank under the counter.

"Nothing." Jeff let his eyes go vague over the symbols. "Not surprising. I studied engineering, not computer science."

"I tried everything I could think of too." Caden poured the resulting pink liquid into two reusable cups and carried them around Jeff's bike trailer. "Here."

Jeff took one of the cups, nodding in thanks. "Maybe I should call IT."

"I wish."

They both peered into the screen.

"Well," Caden said, placing a hand on Jeff's shoulder, "That's enough staring for one day. How about a walk?" He drained his cup and set it on the counter.

Jeff followed him up the ladder and out of the dome. That's what he called it. *Dome.* Did it have another name? Where had it come from?

It took his eyes a moment to adjust. Bright these days. He thought back to right after the Event, when the sky had been clouded over for months, the sun a dim glow. He didn't like to think about it, the way most things had been flattened out of existence. There was no explanation. Only theories. People on the wasteland had all sorts of ideas about what had happened. Everything from rapture to chemical fallout, but nothing hit on all of the effects. The geographical erasure. The absence of bones or rubble. How the land around the surviving patches was only now starting to support life.

He had a theory of his own. This was purgatory. It was the Catholic in him, though he wasn't religious. It was the only parallel he had at hand.

"Anything on your mind?"

"Sorry."

Caden stopped walking. "I'm still getting used to it myself. I wake up and stare at the wall for a while. Then I remember you're next door, and it's a different world, you know?"

"Is it."

Caden followed his gaze to the paper-flat edges curling against their green patch. "Not literally, of course. Everything still happened the way it happened, everything's still the way it was. But for me, it's different."

Jeff nodded slightly. "I know what you mean."

Wind through the field. A faint bird call, maybe a grouse, something earthbound.

"What are those symbols anyway? Maybe a different language? You know, they remind me of QR codes." Caden walked a little ahead and sat down in the grass. Jeff settled next to him, tilting his face to the sun. Caden smiled over at him. "It's a miracle."

"What," Jeff closed his eyes.

"You're relaxed for once."

Jeff laughed in his throat.

"Hey, I get it. I imagine being a Grafter requires constant attention; you're always on the lookout, always watching your back. But there's such a thing as being too careful." Caden brushed some wild strands of hair back from his forehead. "You gotta enjoy it while you have it."

"That's what you do."

"Within reason. These days, I'm only careful when it comes to food." Gently, he reached over and placed his hand on Jeff's. "What about you?"

Jeff looked down at their hands, his expression softening. "I used to be a lot less careful."

"I'd love to hear about it."

Jeff met Caden's eyes, a hollowness deep in his chest. "Maybe some other time."

"Raincheck, then." Caden withdrew his hand. He lay back in the grass, sighing. "It's a fucking beautiful day to be alive."

Brittni Brinn

Chapter 8
Treatment

Symptoms of kidney stones: blood in the urine, intense flank pain
Symptoms of bladder cancer: blood in the urine, discomfort urinating, flank
pain, loss of appetite, anemia

Milo sat next to Pinot on the front steps, waiting for her diagnosis.

"At this point, it could be either."

"I understand."

"I'm sorry."

"I'll have to tell Rhonda. She's still upset I asked you here in the first place."

Pinot only nodded.

"What can I do?"

"Well," Pinot puffed up her cheeks, let out the air in a rush. She tapped a fist on her knee, squinting at the edge of the school lawn. "Couple of options." She stood and went down the three steps onto the grass, as if more comfortable explaining on her feet. "You could wait it out. The kidney stones will pass, but it will be incredibly painful. I can leave you a bottle of painkillers—"

"You have actual painkillers—?"

"But if it's not kidney stones, the cancer will get worse and I'll be too far away to help you."

Milo's mouth tightened into a frown. "If it was...Could you get rid of the cancer?"

"There'd be no way to kill it. Treatment is… palliative at this point. I know some people in Summerland who are trying to figure out how to help with more threatening illnesses, but right now they're mostly concerned with things like tetanus and infection. Those are going to be major problems in the next couple years."

Milo nodded.

"So, here's what we can do…"

***

Rhonda faced one of the empty lockers. Two hands steadied the Canon balanced on her knees, her eyes monitoring the small screen set in the black textured plastic.

She heard Milo's door swing open. He stood in the doorway of his room, waiting for her to turn around. When she didn't, he cleared his throat once, smoothing the back of his hair. "I've decided." His voice depreciated as it jumped against the metal lockers, dissipated into silence.

Rhonda didn't move, her attention tuned into the image on the back of her camera. Inside the locker, a spider climbed arm over arm up a filament thread, its body opalescent. Its insides were clear, nearly invisible. Rhonda waited until the spider had climbed out of the shot. She pressed the red circle, and the screen went dark.

Milo chose treatment. It meant leaving. It meant walking for a long time, it meant possibly dying on the way. But the way he saw it, not leaving was worse.

"I'm staying," Rhonda frowned.

"You'll be alone here. And vulnerable—"

"I'll buy a gun."

"Rhonda."

"My camera's got to be worth a gun, at least." Rhonda got to her feet, slinging the camera strap over her shoulder.

"Pinot tells me the settlement is safe. You can live around people. There are projects to work on, they're—"

"I'll hold down the fort until you come back. Grafters might take it over otherwise."

"Rhonda…" Milo smiled sadly. "I won't be coming back."

"So I should go with you. Watch you die. That sounds so much better."

Milo took a deep breath, his eyes red from lack of sleep. "I would feel a lot better if you came along. I'll… I'll be worried otherwise."

"This is our home. The garden, the caches in the wall. We built all of it. You're asking me to abandon it, like it doesn't matter."

"It's a building." Milo shook his head. "Do you remember how it happened?"

Rhonda fixed her eyes on the blue and grey tiles between her feet.

"We both happened to be here. Nothing more than that. You were editing a film project in the media room. I was getting floor cleaner out of the janitor closet. We happened to be in the surviving corner. That's all. Now, we can move on, keep surviving. It's just a place, Rhonda. We'll find a new place."

Rhonda and Milo both stood in the hall, unable to say anything more. Milo was blinking a lot.

"I don't want to leave you behind," he whispered.

"I don't want you to die."

"How about this: if you come with me, I'll try my best to get better. Okay?"

"Deal." After a moment, she turned away from him and went into her room.

Milo's hands hung limp. One suddenly lifted to press gently on his side. His silence filled each of the lockers flanking him with their emptiness.

***

Rhonda still had a backpack she'd found in one of the lockers. She and Milo had waited a few weeks after the Event before scavenging, just in case someone came back for their stuff. Of course nobody did, and of course Rhonda and Milo stripped the place, hoarding granola bars and trading away backpacks, coats, and shoes too small for them. Their greatest find had been a shopping bag filled with seeds, maybe from an over-zealous biology student, maybe a kid with a green-thumbed parent at home who sent them to pick up gardening supplies. Seeds. All kinds. Vegetables, annuals, perennials. Anything edible, they planted, hidden in the fenced-off plot behind the school. Milo, knowing flowers could draw more than bumblebees, had squirrelled away the extras or traded them off. Rhonda found it stressful, letting go of something so rare.

"We have what we need," Milo would say, "Let someone else enjoy them. Who knows where they'll end up?"

Catching herself smiling at the memory, she quickly twisted her mouth and started packing.

Pinot had told them to take only what they needed. Before anything else, Rhonda wrapped her camera in her crocheted throw and placed it on the soft plastic bottom of the backpack. She piled in her underwear, an extra sweater, her socks. Hopefully, if they got stopped by Grafters, they would think this was only her overnight bag and not dig any deeper. She zipped up the backpack, next opening the mouth of the satchel. She jumbled up the cords she had decided to bring, stuffing them into the satchel along with her laptop. This would be her electronics drop. Messy, the illusion of carelessness. If worse came to worse, she would give the satchel up first. As long as her camera was safe, she could come back from anything.

Her USB, carrying all her footage, as well as the memory card from the camera, she taped onto the inside of her left pant leg, halfway down her calf where the material was loose and would hide the rectangular outlines. She had the camera battery and charger, too; for now, she kept them in her jacket pocket. Easy enough to drop or throw at someone if things got violent.

Fuck, she could feel the knot in her stomach. All those sleepless nights waiting for someone to break in. Now she was making it easy for them. No walls, no blinds to hide her. No cubby in the wall to keep her possessions safe.

The rest of her things were spread out on the counter. Neatly rolled cords, an extra keyboard, headphones, her flip flops, a smear of books and notepads. A couple of knick-knacks, the small model-T someone had kept on display in their locker. It wasn't much, but it was hers.

She hated Milo at that moment. It was his fault they were leaving. Why couldn't they stay? He could get traders to bring in his medicine, they could make movies together and tend the garden, take care of each other like they'd always done. Instead, they were following a stranger to someplace that would probably be cramped and full of people who stole what they needed. Nothing would be safe there. Especially not Milo.

But maybe... maybe there would be someone there...

She picked up that idea with the rest of her possessions and placed them in the wall cubby. She used her bed mat to cover everything evenly. Even if someone did open the wall, they wouldn't see anything of interest right away. She closed the wall panel, taking care to tuck the tab of tape behind it.

One last thing to do. She rolled the soundproofing from her makeshift pillow into a tight cylinder, tied it closed with some twine, and secured it to the top of her backpack.

She straightened up from tying the laces on her old running shoes. "Okay," she said, taking one last look around the room. "Okay."

Brittni Brinn

Chapter 9
Familiar Mystery

The first thing Jeff registered was warmth. On his chest, the hairs on his stomach. He was holding it close to him, his arm gathering it as he rested, his leg wrapped around a limb. A dream, he thought. This body he held was a memory.

He pressed a hand against the warmth, passed over a plain of skin. It could be Kazue, the same hollow chest, the same narrow waist. But he didn't recognize the scent. Kazue always wore cologne, a deep wood infused with citrus, a hint of basil. Even after he showered he smelled the same. But this warmth, it smelled like flour, and grass seed, a hint of sweat.

Jeff opened his eyes. The hair an inch from his face was golden brown, haloed in blue and white light from the screens on the opposite wall. Jeff remembered where he was. He remembered why.

Caden felt him shift and turned over. Jeff relaxed into the single pillow as Caden rested a hand on his chest.

"A fantastic raincheck."

"Sorry for the wait."

Caden closed his eyes slowly, as if to say he didn't mind.

They lay there for a moment in each other's warmth, Jeff with a hand spanning Caden's bare shoulder.

Caden kissed him and rolled out of the single bed. "Breakfast?" He pulled on his pants and stretched his thin arms over his head, walking the step and a half to the kitchenette.

Caden's dome was a mirror image of the dome Jeff had been living in the last few weeks. They were no closer to deciphering the strange symbols but had found other ways to spend their time.

"You need help with anything?" Jeff asked, raising himself on an elbow.

"Relax, man. I got it."

Jeff sunk back into the still-warm bedding, breathing in more of Caden, so he could remember. His eyes wandered up to the screens, letting the sideways symbols lull him with their familiar mystery.

"What the hell?"

"Alright," Caden turned from the counter, "We have instant oatmeal, or I can bake some, what are these, biscuits. Which one sounds better to you?"

"Caden." Jeff waved him over, gaze still locked onto the screen.

Caden laughed as Jeff pulled him down. "Hold on—" Caden crouched beside him, following his gaze to the far wall. "Wait…on the screen, is that—?"

Jeff scrambled over him, crossing the dome in three stumbling steps. He threw himself into the control chair, staring at the red circle that had replaced the four symbols. "Holy shit, holy shit, holy shit!" The red circle glowed around three small words.

Caden was next to him, radiant. "'Press to activate'," he read. The red circle flared at his touch, making way for more circles to appear.

ENGLISH - SPANISH - MANDARIN - ARABIC - JAPANESE…

Caden tapped on the ENGLISH icon.

HELLO, faded onto the screen in its place. WELCOME TO YOUR SURVIVAL UNIT. PLEASE STATE YOUR NAME.

Jeff and Caden stared at the screen. "Caden Stuart," Caden finally replied.

PLEASE CONFIRM THE SPELLING OF YOUR NAME.

Caden laughed at the bolded white letters that appeared below: KADEN STUART. "People always get that wrong." He changed the K to a C.

"What are you doing?"

"Going along with it."

Jeff took a breath and gripped the arms of the padded chair. "Okay…"

THANK YOU.

The words were replaced by a grid of colorful buttons, each featuring a simple pictograph. A radio tower with a notification asterisk next to it, a car wheel. Something that looked like a calculator. There were too many to take in at once.

"So, it's called a Survival Unit?" Caden said, "I wonder where the prior owner ended up."

"I don't even know where to start—this is insane!"

A new circle replaced the grid. It pulsed green around two unbelievable words:

INCOMING MESSAGE.

Before Jeff could say anything, before he could even think about what to do next, Caden reached over his shoulder and tapped the green circle.

As Caden dropped his hand, the circle filled the screen and uploaded an audio link.

"What the hell is it doing now?" Jeff mumbled, salvaging his shirt from the pile of clothes on the floor next to him. The whole thing was getting under his skin, the warmth of bed forgotten.

"Happy death day, Keats." A voice from speakers in the ceiling and behind the screens filled the room. A young voice with sharp edges. "It's been four years now. I should probably stop making these calls, huh? You'd say, it's okay, if they help, keep doing them. But it still wrecks me every time, thinking about you… Heh. Things are fine out here. Didn't find what I was looking for, but that's life, isn't it? Just strange coincidences and the occasional scavenge. Nothing to report. Not much on your end either, I imagine... Anyway... Same time next year?"

Caden was frozen, absorbing the message. Jeff glanced over at him, directing his eyes to the screen.

"What?" Caden whispered.

"Say something."

Caden leaned closer to the screen. "Hello?"

A video window opened, and a man in his early 20s with a black mohawk and the sharpest eye teeth Jeff had ever seen glared out at them. "Who the fuck are you?"

"Nobody," Jeff replied after a moment. "Just passing through."

The young man's eyes flickered off-screen to the left, and then back to Jeff.

"Which one of you's Caden Stuart?"

"That'd be me, hi." Caden waved. "We've been trying to figure this thing out, this Survival Unit?"

"Who's the other one?"

"Nobody," Jeff repeated.

"Okay, 'Nobody', listen up. I don't care that you found this SU. I didn't know there were new residents, that's all. So relax. Actually," the young man's face filled the screen as he leaned in, "it kind of works out for me."

"So about this 'SU'," Caden continued, "how'd it get here, exactly?"

The young man ignored his question. "What about the other one?"

"Who, Jeff?"

"So, Nobody's name is Jeff, thank you Caden." The young man grinned, his teeth gleaming blue and red from what Jeff assumed were the multiple screens on his wall. Was he calling them from another Dome? "But I meant the other SU. There should be two of them."

"What do you mean, it works out for you?" Jeff said, frowning. "Us finding it."

"Heh. Alright, I'll give you something. I've been trying to

retrieve these two SUs for years, but something's fucked up with the homing beacon. The SUs were set to camouflage, maybe that had something to do with it. Whatever it is, I want them, but I need to manually input the coordinates to get them here. Which, I'm unfortunately unable to do. Tough to leave the colony at the moment."

"Colony?" Caden chimed in, "You mean there are more of you?"

"You heard me. We're the safest colony on the west coast."

Jeff shifted in his seat. "You want us to put in the coordinates."

"And come along!" the young man's grin grew larger, "I'd be ever so thankful if you brought these SUs back to me."

"Wait a second," Caden leaned over Jeff's shoulder. "are you telling me these SUs can *move*?"

"We'll have to think about it," Jeff mumbled, gripping the arm of the chair.

"Take all the time you need! But not too much time. I mean, now that you've been inside you know how valuable these SUs are. And I promise, there'd be a place for you in the colony. These machines can last an incredibly long time, and I'm the only one alive who can teach you how to use them properly. So think about it." The young man reached out as if to press something on the screen. "Oh, and by the way, my name's Jax. Call me once you've made your decision."

"One more question," Caden cut in, his hazel eyes serious. "Who was your message supposed to be for?"

Jax glared at him, then eased his expression into a grin. "Nobody."

Chapter 10
Journey

Rhonda peered through the darkness around them, listening. She didn't really know what to watch for. Pinot had said lights, engines, footsteps, anything, but she'd been awake forever, and nothing had changed. Had it been two hours or three? She found the big dipper, Ursa Major, balanced on its handle. The points gleamed through the faint cloud of her breath. A couple more weeks, and it would be too cold to traverse these wide empty lands.

She was sitting up, the soundproofing barely cushioning her from the hard ground beneath. Pinot's back was towards her, radiating heat. Milo slept face up, his arms tucked underneath his rough wool blanket. Rhonda could hear their breathing, make out the outlines of their bodies resting on either side of her legs.

She felt for her satchel underneath the blanket draped over her knees. The hard plastic case of her laptop was cool to the touch. Everything was alright. Still, she could hear her heart in her ears, the dryness of her mouth. She wasn't used to sleeping outside, the extreme vulnerability that had kept her awake the entire first night out in the wasteland. But nothing had happened to them.

Only four more days until they arrived. They were going to make it.

"Where are we going, exactly?" she'd asked Pinot as they were leaving the school. Milo had locked the door, out of habit, though they both knew it would do little good. From now on, this was a place that used to be.

"It's kind of a restaurant," Pinot had replied.

"A restaurant."

"There's about twenty people living there."

Rhonda had caught her breath at that. Twenty people living in one place was as unbelievable as a miracle.

"Arissa runs it, you'll meet her when we get there. Though, I don't think she was expecting two more residents. Milo's message was 'I need a doctor.' No mention of you, smart. But don't worry, she'll like you. You're not hiding anything."

A sudden noise startled Rhonda back to her place between Milo and Pinot, where the edges of her body were starting to go numb. Her senses swept the deeper dark of the wasteland, and the sound came again, but it was only Milo shifting in his sleep. He mumbled something, rolled onto his side. "Rhonda?"

"Why, hello there!" she said in an obnoxiously cheerful voice.

A resulting groan that could've doubled as a reluctant laugh. "If being on watch is making you that happy, maybe I'd better take my turn."

Rhonda stood up as Milo shuffled into the spot she'd been warming for the past few hours. She took her bags with her, using the backpack as a pillow, the satchel under the crook of her knees. Milo's torso was grey against the starry backdrop, and even though she couldn't make out much of his face, she could sense his mild smile as he draped her crocheted blanket across her stomach. "Night, my dear."

"I'm still mad at you."

"Have a good sleep."

A yawn cracked open her jaw. "Night, old man." Rhonda crossed her arms into her sleeves, breathed deep into her stomach and counted stars until she drifted into sleep.

Chapter 11
On Foot

Pinot was feeling the last leg of the journey. She paused at the edge of the forest, letting the pain in her feet travel up into her calves. "Time for a break," she called back to Milo and Rhonda. She crouched, stretching her soles and sighing in relief as her knees cracked. She unhitched her backpack, a hand catching her hood as the strap pulled it down. Milo and Rhonda caught up to her. Rhonda wore a baggy navy windbreaker and sweatpants, and had her hair tucked up into a toque. Milo was in work jeans and a nylon vest over a thick beige sweater. They were nondescript enough to pass by most places unbothered. So far, they hadn't run into a single Grafter, and for that, Pinot was grateful.

"Here," Pinot handed Milo a water bottle from her pack. She also slipped him a single capsule, which he immediately downed. The fewer resources they showed off, the less likely they'd be followed.

"Aren't you being a little paranoid?" Rhonda had asked their first day out from the school. Pinot had explained the necessity of hiding their hair and figures—lots of starved people wandering the wasteland these days, and not just for food. Still, Rhonda was not happy about leaving her snug wool coat behind in favor of the baggy windbreaker.

"You want to get there in one piece, don't you?" Pinot had

said, lightly enough. Even then she'd been gripping the handle of her switchblade, forever hidden in the deep left pocket of her hoodie. She'd been lucky, getting to Milo: the traders who had delivered his message had traveled with her halfway, but the last three days she'd been in the wasteland alone, and that was an experience she was not interested in repeating.

They'd made it to the edge of the forest, at least. When the haze of green had appeared on the horizon, Pinot had let out a breath she hadn't realized she'd been holding. The forest was hard to miss, but there was always the chance that her compass had gone wonky, or that she'd gotten turned around in the endless wasteland.

"We've got about two days of walking left." Pinot took a swig from Milo's water bottle and wiped her mouth on her wrist, before rubbing the moisture left behind on her wrist tattoo onto her cargo pants. She handed Rhonda the bottle, who grimaced before taking a small sip. "A little bit of spit's not going to hurt you," Pinot deadpanned. She recapped the bottle and hiked her pack onto her shoulders as she stood. "I'll find us a camping spot for the night. Be right back." Milo nodded weakly. He didn't look good, a grey pallor under his skin. Pinot decided to give them an extra hour of sleep the next morning, in the hopes they'd make better time picking their way through the woods.

She found a small clearing about ten minutes into the forest. No water nearby, but they'd stumble onto the creek soon enough. Pinot was heading back through the trees when she heard voices. She took off running towards the shouting, which was coming from where she'd left Milo and Rhonda.

There were three of them, ragged Grafters with dirty clothes and greasy hair. One wore a pair of wire-rimmed glasses. Another was holding Rhonda's satchel. The third pointed a makeshift spear at Milo's throat.

"Hey!" Pinot drew their attention, keeping her stance even and her voice steady. Only the one with glasses looked up.

"Oh good, one more," the Grafter re-adjusted his frames. "I wonder what's in your backpack. Let's take a look." He motioned for the spear-woman to take Pinot's bag, which is exactly what Pinot wanted.

"I'm a doctor," she said as the woman approached. "Can I take a look at your injury?"

The woman narrowed her eyes at Pinot. "This one says she's a doctor." She shot a quick glance, almost a glare, at the Grafter holding Rhonda's satchel.

The Grafter wearing glasses considered Pinot, a mocking grin on his face. "A doctor, huh?"

Pinot took her hands slowly from her pockets. "It's starting to look infected." The woman's arm was scratched up, crossed over in deep slashes. "Looks like you ran into something pretty nasty."

The woman shrugged.

Pinot eased down, "I'm going to take out some supplies to treat your wound. Is that okay?"

The man with the glasses grimaced. "Slowly."

Unhooking one of her arms from her backpack, Pinot unzipped her bag and took out a full water bottle, a roll of gauze and a container of homemade painkillers. The woman handed her spear to the man with the glasses and pulled her short tattered sleeve clear of the wounds.

Pinot shook the bottle, a slight foam forming on the surface of the water. She dribbled it slowly over the woman's bare arm. She recapped the half-empty water bottle, sparing a quick look to Rhonda and Milo.

"Here," Pinot handed the water bottle to the other Grafter, the one with Rhonda's satchel. "Don't lose that." She ripped the plastic cover from the gauze with her teeth and used a couple of pre-cut lengths to seal the spear-woman's arm. "Okay," Pinot said next, handing her the rest of the gauze, "This is important." Pinot secured her backpack, stood up, and brushed the dust from her knees. "Tomorrow at about this time, unwrap the wound and do exactly what I just did. Wrap it up and leave it on for a week, and by then, the cuts should be clean of infection."

Pinot approached the man with the glasses, handing him the

white plastic pill container. "She needs to take one painkiller, just one, each night before she goes to sleep. For a week, that's all. There are more than enough in there, so if any of the rest of you run into barbed wire, or whatever it was," she sent a pointed look at the man holding Rhonda's satchel, "you can take them."

None of the Grafters responded; they stared at the materials Pinot had given them as if remembering her instructions. She walked quietly past the man with the glasses, gathered up Rhonda and Milo, and assuredly, though quickly, led them into the forest.

"My bag—" Rhonda started to say, but Pinot gripped her arm so tightly she didn't continue.

"Whatever was in there is gone," Pinot said after a minute of forested silence. "You and Milo, on the other hand, are still here."

They picked their way through the darkening woods, Pinot leading them in random angles and occasionally stopping to listen for followers. They heard no one. They did not sleep. They walked all night.

Book Two

Chapter 1
May

Empty window frame. Double layer of plastic duct-taped over the gaping hole. Rain tapping, wind slapping, stretching the outer layer in towards the second. Outside, the sound of branches creaking overhead.

May stood by the cabin sink, holding Lucas in her arms. He was wrapped up, asleep, his face cushioned inside her old college sweater.

"Hey there, little one," she said as he opened his eyes. They were like Isak's, dark brown, but with shots of bronze starbursting from his serious pupils. He yawned. "You're up late. Can't sleep?"

She walked him around the kitchen table, but he didn't settle, straining inside of his wrap.

"Alright, alright. Hold on a second."

Isak was stretched out on the couch. It couldn't have been much past midnight, but the storm had lulled him to sleep, just as it had startled her awake. May carried Lucas around Isak, careful to step gently on the rough wooden floorboards. One creaked slightly, the sound blending into the raindrops streaking the front windowpane.

May reached Isak's old blue and green quilt, a tattered rectangle spread across the floor. She loosened the sweater around Lucas and set him on the feeble padding. Wiggling his body, the sweater fell away. Lucas wore a faded set of spaceship pajamas; one of his feet disappeared into the ankle cuff as he strove towards the opposite side of the quilt, the window, and the rattling of the storm outside.

"What's this? Hey, hey. Look." May set down a stuffed dinosaur made from an old set of pants that Isak had worn through at the knees. She'd used extra buttons from her jean jacket for eyes. The little dino danced and Lucas changed his path, listing his head as he half crawled, half squiggled over to it.

"There you go." May let him push the toy out of her hands. She looked up at the window which was covered in silver spots, streaks of rain over the glass. It was cool in the cabin, but comfortably so. She gritted her teeth at the thought of fall; soon they'd have to pack up, head to Arissa's. The past four winters had gotten progressively colder, as if the world was taking its time to remember what seasons were. Last winter was the first they'd had to leave the cabin. Definitely not a time May remembered fondly.

Lucas, tired of the stuffed animal, reached up.

"Hungry?"

May lifted Lucas with her as she settled into their armchair and fed him until he fell asleep.

The slow heaviness of time wrapped around her. The rain continued, uncountable water drops hitting uncountable leaves, dripping into uncountable puddles…

Isak suddenly appeared beside her, as if he had been standing there for a long time, a hand resting on her shoulder. But he hadn't been there, he hadn't placed his hand. He'd skipped the time between the couch and his place between her and the window.

"It's really coming down out there," he said.

"Did the storm wake you up?"

"No," he pushed back the black hair that tumbled over his eyes. "I just wanted to see you."

May crossed her free hand over to his. Her other hand kept

a firm hold of Lucas.

Isak's ragged brown housecoat was tied over his sweater and sweatpants, his feet bulky under two layers of socks. He shifted his weight, bending his knees to take the strain off his old leg injury. "I was thinking, we should leave sooner than later. It's already getting cold."

May sighed. "We still have a lot to organize here. Did you pack all of the summer clothes in the bin yesterday?"

"It's ready to go. Just got to bury it in the back, and we'll be all set."

May looked up past Isak, her eyes running over the rough wooden walls, the shelf of old jars and dusty knick-knacks the previous owners had left behind. "It's going to be hard this year."

"I know." Isak reached down and freed Lucas's foot from his pajamas.

The sound of rain filled the space between them, the storm giving way to a light pattering on the roof, and then silence.

Brittni Brinn

Chapter 2
Ulway

Theodore Ulway hated being called Theodore. He much preferred being called by his last name, Ulway. If someone bothered to ask why, he wouldn't tell them. He simply preferred Ulway, and that was that.

Ulway, then, was the first to spot the three people coming up the dirt road that led to the restaurant. A man with grey hair, a tall young lady, and Pinot, who was scowling. He already knew Pinot, as she'd lived at the restaurant for almost four years, but he didn't know why she was scowling. His aunt Arissa came up beside him, waving at Pinot and the newcomers.

"We were so close to making it without any trouble," Pinot told Arissa as they walked together through the giant double doors. "Grafters, on the edge of the forest..." Ulway fell behind, looking up at the big sign set above the door, which read *Ulway's Restaurant & Retreat Centre*. Ulway's mom and dad used to run the restaurant until they went away. Then everything else went away. The Event, everyone called it. That's why there was a wasteland surrounding their forest, why most people had disappeared. His aunt always told him that his parents could still be alive somewhere, but it had been five years and there had been no sign of them. They could've made it to Timbuktu by now, Ulway thought to himself. He used to think 'Timbuktu' was just a word that sounded funny, but he looked it up in one of his mom's old encyclopedias and there was a map of the world and Timbuktu was on it.

He caught up to Arissa and Pinot and the new people in the dining hall.

"I hope you're keeping your aunt out of trouble, Ulway." Pinot reached up to punch him gently on the shoulder and he punched her back. Their way of saying hello.

"I try," he whispered. Then he coughed a little. On the best days, Ulway's voice was raspy, and hurt him if he talked too much. Before she left a few weeks ago, Pinot told him to drink warm water with honey mixed in, so he tried to do that even though Pinot wasn't really a doctor. She told Ulway once that she felt more like a healer, which made sense to him since she could actually heal people with her spit. The Event did stuff like that to people. To him, too.

"Theodore," his aunt said, and he frowned sharply at the sound of his first name, "this is Milo and Rhonda. They're going to be staying here for a while."

He waved shyly and managed a hello, and they said hello back. Ulway liked Milo right away. An older man with a quiet smile. Rhonda was tall with round cheeks and had all of her hair in a toque so he didn't know what colour it was. Her eyebrows were black, though, and he thought that head hair was usually around the same colour as a person's eyebrows.

They gathered around one of the tables in the dining hall, talking about where everyone would sleep and how chores worked, where the bathroom was. Ulway knew the restaurant had 40 round tables in total, but most of them were folded up and put away in the closet because there were only 22 residents. The five tables they needed to seat everyone were clustered near the front of the dining hall. They were all set for dinner, which reminded Ulway that he had something important to do.

He made his way around the new people to stand by his aunt. "I'm going to start," he whispered and cleared his throat.

"I'll be there to help in a couple of minutes." His aunt placed a hand on his bulky shoulder, the shoulder he didn't really like because sometimes it ached or was painful to sleep on. Pinot couldn't heal that, Ulway knew, but she did tell him to try and stretch once a day so the muscles wouldn't get tight. And he tried to do that too, because Pinot knew how to take care of people.

His aunt gave a couple more instructions and then led Milo down a small hallway to the clinic. Pinot disappeared down the nearby flight of stairs.

Ulway pushed through the swinging door into the kitchen. He could still see Rhonda because there was no wall between them, only a wide counter. She picked up a fork from one of the place settings and put it back. Ulway wondered what she liked to eat and then thought about what he liked to eat, and as he set a massive pot of water on the stove, wondered if they liked to eat the same things. He watched as Pinot came back upstairs without her backpack. She said something to Rhonda and then turned down the hall. Ulway wondered if Milo was sick.

The door swept open and his aunt burst into the kitchen. "What are we having tonight?" she asked cheerfully.

"Spaghetti!" He released a few more handfuls of pasta into the pot and watched it until it boiled.

Brittni Brinn

Chapter 3
Blue Flame

Left alone in the dining room, Rhonda wound her way through the tables, each complete with plastic placemats framing one fork, one knife, and a spoon. She reached the wooden railing along the side wall. A set of stairs descended along it. She paused on the first step and squinted down the corridor Arissa had taken Milo down. The clinic's at the end of that hallway, she thought. After a moment, she continued down the stairs.

The windowless hallway at the bottom was illuminated by a mounted LED strip that ran along the walls and over a few doorframes on each side. An open doorway on the left caught her attention. Blue-tinged light drew her, familiar from her many hours alone in the media classroom.

She drifted in quietly, a moth to blue flame. The room was cramped, likely a repurposed closet. A scaffold-like shelving unit took up the whole of one wall, overflowing with cords and wires, some tacked along the floor, some disappearing under a ceiling panel. Most of them, however, led to the computer desk and the figure sitting at it, silhouetted by the monitor in front of them. As she approached, the screen grew clearer and she could make out a grid with a small sprite in the middle of it.

"An RPG?" she exclaimed, then started as the figure turned to face her. "Are you building an RPG?"

The figure leaned to the far side of the monitor and flicked a switch. An overhead fluorescent hummed to life. A man settled back into the chair. His hair was red and disheveled, his eyes grey-blue and lively in his drawn face. He tilted his head at the monitor and nodded.

Rhonda examined the image filling the computer screen: a simple 8-bit graphic of a knight standing in a field ringed with blocky mountains.

The man opened a chat window.

You're new.

"I'm Rhonda," she replied, "Just got here."

I'm Ed, he typed. *You came in with Pinot?*

Noticing Ed's eyes on her, Rhonda nodded.

Sorry about your dad. Pinot told me he's pretty sick.

"Yeah." She dug her hand deep in her pocket, looking for something to hold onto.

You're not going to find a better doctor, not anywhere, he continued. *You can trust her.*

Rhonda found the camera battery in the depths and gripped until the square edges cut into her finger joints. "What about you?" Rhonda asked, "What do you do around here?"

Ed sat back in his office chair until the springs creaked. He held up a hand, indicating the wires, the multiple computer towers lined up on the bottom row of the shelving unit.

"You run a server?"

Ed gave her a thumbs up, and pointed to where a thick snake of cords ran up through the ceiling.

"For the whole building, that's cool."

He fit his fingers back onto the keyboard. *Just a message board and this video game. Not quite up to pre-Event standards, but it's something.*

"It's amazing," Rhonda said.

I'll set up a log in for you.

Ed closed out of the RPG, opening a new window. A black rectangle filled with blocky white letters came up on the screen. Ed positioned the cursor and started typing. After a couple of lines of what looked like gibberish to Rhonda, his fingers stilled and he looked up at her, waiting. She squinted at the small type. Ed had the cursor positioned after SCREEN NAME.

Rhonda smiled. "TheRealRhonda. It's not taken is it? Or should I add a number to the end?"

Ed didn't make a sound, but a glance told her that he was laughing. He typed 'TheRealRhonda37' and bumped the cursor down to PASSWORD. He turned his chair to face the door as she input a four-digit code.

"Okay, done," Rhonda said, reluctantly relinquishing the keyboard.

Ed pressed the Enter key with a final flourish. The monitor flickered for a moment, then presented a smaller text window overtop, reading SUCCESS.

"Now what? How do I get in?"

Ed transitioned to another chat window. *You can use any of the monitors upstairs. This one's for admin purposes, so it's off limits. Press the on button and wait for the sign in screen to prompt you.*

"Can I…? I have a USB, can I transfer some files onto the system? Do I have a permanent account?"

Suddenly, the overhead light, the monitor, and the hum of the computer bank cut out.

"Power outage?" Rhonda asked through the dark.

A moment later, the light flickered back on. Ed's eyes were closed. The computer bank hummed and the monitor loaded the start-up screen.

"Ed? Are you okay?"

His eyelids flickered open, and he stared at Rhonda for a moment before returning to the keyboard. He typed in a few commands and reopened their chat window.

You said you had a USB?

"Yeah, but—"

I'll have to check it first. Bring it down tomorrow. Sorry. Long day.

Rhonda followed him out of the room, closing the door behind her. Ed stumbled up the stairs and was gone. The hum of the computer towers faded behind her as she continued down the hallway and entered the next door on her right.

There was an empty camping cot closest to the door, all ready for her just as Arissa had promised. Realizing that she was exhausted, she stuffed her backpack down to the bottom of the bed, kicked off her shoes, climbed under the thick wool blanket, and fell fully and deeply asleep.

Chapter 4
Pinot

Cross-legged on her bed, Pinot buttoned up her flannel shirt. With her hoodie zipped over top, she had three layers, plus her ragged cargo pants and thick wool socks. Usually, it was enough to keep her from climbing back into her warm bed. There was a wood-burning fireplace in the dining area upstairs, but no sense of central heating, and the extremities of the building suffered from a constant chill. Maybe in the old days, Ed could've kept some heaters going while he was holed up in his office, but not anymore. He was wearing out, like she was. Their abilities were starting to break up: power outages and no more miraculous healings.

Every couple of weeks, she'd make a small cut in the back of her hand with her switchblade. Spit in the red, swab it away. Then take notes of how long it took to heal, administering spit every 2 hours. There was a definite drop in the effectiveness of what before could heal any wound in a matter of minutes. Now it would take days.

After pulling on her hiking boots, she tread quietly between the cots and couches and rickety beds full of sleeping residents. It was barely past dawn, but she headed to the clinic. A room up the stairs, through the dining room, down a small hall, to the right of the emergency exit. Her right hand searched her hoodie pocket, pushing aside her fingerless glove and closing around her keys. Unlocking the clinic door, she smirked a little. The handle lock was so basic a four-year-old with a bobby pin could spring it.

The room was small, with space for a couple of chairs and a padded bench. A single-paned window let in enough light to be able to do without artificial substitutes for most of the day. She had a counter too, the back lined with jars of bandages, gauze, cotton swabs, along with a container of tweezers, scissors, and a thermometer soaking in disinfectant. Secured in a locked cupboard underneath were her pill-making supplies; she usually spent an hour each morning putting pills together, thin capsules filled with a mixture of olive oil and her spit, bottling them to hand out in the case of flu outbreaks or to pass on to traders. Maybe only placebos now.

Instead of taking out the half capsules and bottle of olive oil (god knew where Arissa sourced these rarities from), Pinot sat in one of the clinical chairs, leaning on the back legs so that her shoulders rested against the wall. It was a slow kind of feeling, the day just starting, the sounds of people downstairs starting to wake up, closing doors and exchanging good mornings, muffled by the wooden floor.

Pinot gripped the handle of her switchblade, eternally in her left pocket, something to ground her before she flew off. Who knew where? There were many other wheres now, not just the single-person patches she would stumble onto in the wasteland. Places where people ate, slept, shared stories. People came together. The relative tendency for matter to move towards other matter. She could see it here, at the restaurant, in the trading caravans that made regular stops, the way they were more than the sum of their parts. Some kind of social gravity—

Pinot snapped out of her thoughts, startled by the figure standing in the doorway.

"I didn't mean to disturb you," Arissa smiled. The past four years had brought her fully into middle age, streaks of grey in her naturally crimped black hair, a healthy weight setting into her cheeks. She wore a loose grey sweater, sky blue pants gathered at her ankles, and moccasins, the same ones she had been wearing the night Pinot had first arrived at her strange restaurant.

"Just thinking." Pinot grounded the chair legs and offered Arissa the bench.

She held up a hand in gentle refusal. "I'm on my way to the kitchen. Can I bring you something?"

"Don't worry about it. I'll make an appearance later."

"Really?" Arissa's dark eyes sparkled. "You never have breakfast with the rest, always before, or after. I wonder what's changed your mind…"

"It's just breakfast."

Arissa winked as she left the doorway, her soft footsteps fading down the hall.

Pinot rolled her head in a half circle. She knew Arissa could read her feelings, though like her own fading ability, it was less potent than it used to be. Still, Arissa sensed that Pinot was interested in the new arrivals. So what? She liked Milo, and Rhonda was the same age as her. It was nice to have new people around. Most of the residents at the restaurant had come to see Pinot as their doctor and nothing more. She'd tried to befriend some of them, but there wasn't that feeling. Not like she'd had with the Partier, Eliot. Not like the connection she'd had with Jax.

She kicked off from the chair, crouching down to unlock the cupboard. Instead of reaching for the bag of pill supplies, she took out a tattered softcover textbook, featuring a human body with its muscles and tissue exposed. Sitting on the countertop, she flipped to a random page and started listing the names of hand bones. *Distal phalanges, middle phalanges, proximal phalanges, hamate, triquetral, carpus…*

She resurfaced about an hour later. Chatter from the dining room wafted in through her open door. Breakfast was ready. Arissa usually set up for the meal, while various volunteers would take care of lunch and dinner. Pinot preferred to be on dishes duty, often taking other people's turns so she wouldn't have to cook. She liked her food mysterious, liked that it arrived without her quite knowing how. And she was thankful that she would never have to cook like that for anyone, because cooking was commitment. And you could really mess that up.

Locking the handle, Pinot shut the clinic door and headed to the dining hall. If anyone needed a patch up, they wouldn't have to look far to find her. She dug into her pockets, pushing the closed-up knife and her key ring down to the bottom, resting her fingerless gloves up near the mouths.

A handful of people sat at the round tables, more stood in a small cluster around the breakfast buffet with half-full plates. Pinot made straight for the counter that connected the kitchen to the dining room, a wide proscenium-like opening framing the industrial sinks and countertops within.

Picking up the carafe of instant coffee, she poured herself a cup, watching the semi-brown liquid stream through the air. The initial impact of coffee on the ceramic, then the satisfying sound of it increasing, until the coffee hit the brim and she relented. There was a jar full of powdered creamer, but Pinot hated the smell. Instead, she made do with a bit of honey to take the edge off the bitter instant coffee. Something stronger would've saved her the entire cream conundrum, but liquor was hard to come by.

Nothing was easy like it had been in the age of light switches and tap water. They all had to make sacrifices, learn to live together, live without.

"Gooooood morning, Pinot!"

"Nick," she said without turning from the absorbing task of stirring her coffee. The spoon clicked against the insides of the mug, standing in for any further reply.

Nick leaned his elbows on the counter next to her, trying to catch her eye. "How'd you sleep last night? It was pretty cold, I had to borrow an extra blanket."

"Oh yeah?" she said tonelessly, placing the spoon in the cup marked DIRTY.

"Hey, I'm really glad you're back." Nick's elbow grazed hers.

"It's been awhile since we spent quality time together. Wanna do something tonight?"

Pinot picked up her mug of coffee and blew across the top. The stream dissipated, revealing the faces and yawns of the morning crowd. "Sure."

"Great!" Nick ran a hand through his hair. "I'll see you later then. Same time and place?"

Pinot stiffened her body to stave off any further contact, but Nick had already gone over to sit with his friends Stef and Markus.

She watched them for a moment. How easy they made it seem, just to be there. Sitting together, laughing over something stupid. They were so fucking shallow. Nick most of all. He washed his hair every fucking day, even though they were supposed to conserve resources as much as possible. He used perfumed soap for fuck's sake. Didn't matter that it smelled amazing. Didn't matter that his elaborate personal hygiene rituals made sex with him bearable. *Now who's being shallow?* She pushed down a desire to vomit.

She took a sip of the coffee, letting it scald her tongue. Might as well get this over with, she thought, and made her way to the table where Milo and Rhonda were sitting. Even though she'd spent a couple weeks with them already, it was strange to see them here. Like, in the old days, when you'd see a cashier from the corner store at a party. You'd recognize them, but it would take a while to place where from. Sitting at the table Pinot had probably sat at hundreds of times, they were as foreboding as strangers.

"Is, uh, mind if I sit with you?" Pinot asked.

"Take your pick," Milo smiled. He finished setting his watch, matching the hands to the clock hanging above the kitchen door.

Pinot sat in one of the chairs between him and Rhonda. "So, what do you think?"

"Of this place?" Rhonda asked. She took a bite of toast. "It's okay."

The corners of Milo's mouth lowered a miniscule degree.

"Rhonda, you were just saying you can't remember the last time you had bread."

"Pinot knows what I think about coming here. I'm not going to offend her."

The rest of the smile drained out of Milo's face. "It'll just take some time to get used to it."

"Who are all these people, anyway?" Rhonda said, sweeping her toast at the room. "Grafters?"

Pinot shrugged. "They come through, some stay for a while, some leave. Mostly from the patches around here, once they ran out of supplies, looking for a place to stay."

"How long have you been here?" Milo asked.

"Four years."

"You stayed, so I guess it's not that bad?"

"Yeah, not bad." Pinot found Nick across the room. He was eating through a mound of dry cereal, laughing as Stef threw an arm around Markus. "Most of the time."

Taking a sip of her coffee, Pinot noticed a bright red mess of hair over the stair railing. The rest of Ed soon followed, a thin stick of a human, his shoulders bowed in under one of the restaurant's standard-issue wool blankets. It was strange to see him before noon. Ed was a late sleeper on his best days, and the way his foot caught on the last step was enough of a clue that even now he wasn't really awake.

Paying no attention to the food offered at the breakfast buffet, Ed listed in the direction of their table. He fell into the seat across from Pinot and gave them all a cursory glance, followed by his usual nervous smile.

"What the hell are you doing up so early?" Pinot said, concerned with the way his cheeks bowed inwards.

He shrugged a little, flicked his eyes over to Rhonda.

"Good morning to you too," Rhonda responded. She opened the left panel of her windbreaker and fished a USB out of the inside pocket. "Is this what you're looking for?"

Ed indicated he'd look at it later with a laid-back hand wave. He turned to Milo, raised his eyebrows.

"Milo," Milo held out a hand. Ed shook it and settled deeper in his chair, closing the blanket over his threadbare t-shirt and pajama pants. "You don't talk much, do ya?"

Pinot got the go ahead from Ed and explained. "He hasn't said a word in five years. The Event changed some things about him."

Rhonda looked up from her second piece of toast. "What kind of things?"

One of the overhead lights came on and flashed twice. Rhonda and Milo stared at it in wonder.

"Don't worry," Victoria called over from the table next to them, "Ed's just showing off." And she waved at Pinot before turning back to her breakfast.

Ed winked and got up from the table. Hearing his breath wheeze in his chest, Pinot shot him a look, but he shook his head in a way that said he was fine. He started shuffling in the direction of the stairs.

"Wait a minute—" Rhonda said, but he interrupted by spinning around and holding up 7 fingers, three on his right hand and 4 on his left. Then, he descended.

"He means 7 pm," Pinot explained, draining the rest of her coffee. "That's when you'll see what he can really do." She stood up and pushed in her chair, grimacing as she felt the distance between them and her return. She was still the doctor, after all. "Milo, I'd like to see you this afternoon. I'll be in the clinic if you need me." And she left the dining hall without another word.

Chapter 5
Evening

At 7 pm, all the lights turned on. The churning sound of a dishwasher started up in the kitchen, and music wafted down the hall from the far bedroom. The three computer monitors on the far side of the dining room glowed.

Rhonda was heading to Ed's office when everything came to life. "This is all you?" she asked him without saying hello.

Ed sat facing the door, his eyes closed. He nodded.

"Huh. With a generator or what?"

Ed opened his eyes and the screen behind him went dark. He held up his hands, showing them to be empty. When he blinked the screen turned on.

"But... you're controlling it... with your mind?"

The brightness in the room increased then returned to normal.

"I thought all the stories about... powers... caused by the Event were, you know, bullshit."

Ed shrugged and turned to his monitor. *Got your USB ready?* he typed.

Rhonda handed it to him, and he plugged it into the front of one of the computer towers.

What you got on here? He scrolled through a long readout.

"Some short videos I made," she said. "Nothing bad."

Used this USB on any other computers?

"Just my laptop."

Ed raised his eyebrows at her but she shook her head. "I don't have it anymore."

Too bad.

After a few more moments, Ed closed the info window, unplugged the USB, and handed it back to her.

Looks good, he typed in the chat box. *You can use it on any of the computers upstairs.*

"Thanks."

What kinds of videos?

Rhonda felt her palms get sweaty. "Nothing much. Short films. Kind of day to day stuff, you know."

Are you going to make more?

"I mean, I want to, but…"

But what?

"It's still too new here. Maybe once I get a feel for the place first."

He shrugged as if to say 'cool'. *Gotta concentrate,* he typed next.

"Sure, thanks Ed." She turned back in the doorway, waving goodnight, but his eyes were closed again. The fluorescents hummed above her all the way up to the dining hall.

***

Pinot felt more than saw the lights turn on. She was lying on her bed fully clothed, *The Catcher in the Rye* open on her stomach. She didn't feel much like reading. Holden was about to ask the taxi driver about ducks and she always felt sad at that particular section. She'd read the book dozens of times over the past four years; she didn't know why she kept going back to it. It was about some whiny rich kid trying to come to terms with how messed up the world was. At least it gave her a break from the biology textbooks and old medical journals. Pinot was a high school drop-out and here she was playing doctor. But there was no one else. She was the closest thing they had.

Thinking back on her meeting with Milo that afternoon, she felt a pit dig itself into her stomach. She'd invited him to come in and sit down, asked about how he was settling in, if Rhonda was doing okay. She'd asked him about his discomfort and if he noticed any changes since arriving. He'd said he just felt tired from the week-long walk from the school building. That's to be expected, Pinot had replied. She'd given him a bottle of pills, telling him to take one before bed every night with a small glass of water. She advised no coffee and no sugar. She let him know that she was always available to meet with him and was around the clinic most days from right after breakfast until lunch, and then from mid-afternoon until just before the lights came on at 7. Milo had taken it all of it pretty well, but as he was easing up out of the chair, he asked if there really wasn't anything else they could do.

"Not right now," Pinot had said, trying to keep her tone even. "I'll let you know if other options come up."

Milo had nodded and left, starting to whistle as he exited into the hallway.

And there was nothing else she could do. Not here. Not with the limited supplies and knowledge she had. Healing people with your spit was one thing. Cutting them open to remove a source of pain—that was another thing entirely.

"Shit." She suddenly remembered that it was lights-on, which meant that Nick would be expecting her. Swinging her legs off the bed, she tucked Salinger under her pillow, tied half of her hair up with an elastic band, and headed to the back door.

"And where are you going in such a hurry?" Sophie asked her from the next bed over.

Pinot started, caught mid-stride. She'd thought she was alone in the room, expecting most people to be out of the dorms and into the common area for the two hours of power they would have all day.

"Out for a walk. I go crazy cooped up in here" she laughed, hoping Sophie would buy it.

"Oh, me too honey." Sophie was wearing a nightcap over her grey braids, and had her blanket pulled up to her chin. "You have a good time."

Pinot sighed as the back door closed behind her. Not that she had to use this door. But the thought of having to walk upstairs, through the clusters of people standing in line to use the computers or playing cards, asking her where she was going, telling her about their headaches or the trouble they were having falling asleep—it was too much. She was already having second thoughts about seeing Nick. Still, she couldn't help but jog through the shadowy trees, hoping that she wasn't too late.

He was waiting by the douglas fir they'd carved their initials in earlier that year, a stupid romantic gesture that made her sick every time she thought about it.

"It's beautiful out here. A little cold, but I brought an extra blanket." Nick beamed, and she couldn't help but smile back. He was happy, she realized. It wasn't his hair that she was attracted to. Despite everything, Nick was an unironically happy person.

Pinot helped him lay out one of the blankets before joining him underneath the second. "We have to find a new meeting place," she told him, "it's fucking freezing out here."

Chapter 6
New Arrivals

Pinot could hear them from down the hall—Nick, Stef and Markus, Sophie, and the other residents whose names and medical conditions she could rattle off without thinking. Something unusual was happening around the main entryway. She moved closer to the voices and shut the clinic door behind her, curious. It was still weeks until the next trading caravan was scheduled to stop by. A new arrival, maybe?

As Pinot reached the edge of the group, some of the heads shifted and she saw through the resulting window what, or rather who, everyone was so excited to see. She spun around and headed back down the hallway, gritting her teeth until they started to ache. She didn't loosen the grip on her switchblade until she'd locked herself in the clinic.

The padded bench did little to cushion her against the cold hard fact that they were back. She should have expected it. The nights were close to freezing and a general cough was developing, some of the older residents starting to show signs of mild bronchial infection. Arissa had already cleared out one of the storage rooms to use as a sick bay for the more serious patients, as they had during a flu outbreak the previous winter. And now it was almost winter again, and May was back. Except this time, she had a baby with her.

Bringing a kid into this germ pool? Come on, May, use your head.

Maybe it'd be good, her brain countered, exposure could build up his immune system; but if something went wrong, Pinot had no idea what she could do. The kid wasn't inoculated against anything. No booster shots for children of the apocalypse.

Against her better judgement, she thought back to last December and May's long labour. When Sophie and Arissa had finally brought Lucas out, crying and healthy, Pinot had been there to cut the umbilical cord and wrap him in a clean towel. She'd sat up that first night with Lucas to make sure he kept breathing. Watching him, she'd felt ecstatic and depressed; most of all, she was excited for him to grow up and live. Still, she didn't regret offering to help end May's pregnancy seven months before, even though May had never, and would never, forgive her for it.

Lucas had been born. He breathed, and cried, and slept. Pinot's healing abilities had helped May get through the worst of the labor and the pain afterwards. But right before May left the makeshift infirmary, she'd turned to Pinot, her arms rigid around her bundled infant. "You wanted me to get rid of him. Never touch him again." Pinot could picture the woman's face as her mouth formed around the words: her cheeks bleached white from the hours of labor, her long black hair plastered to her forehead, damp with sweat. She'd wanted to tell May that she only wanted to help, that she was happy for them, that she could do even more now that Lucas had been born. But something cracked open inside of her then, and from that moment on, everything that she could hate about May, she did.

Pinot pushed it away, the labor, Lucas—She couldn't change anything about that now.

Instead, she fell into thinking about making flu shots out of her tears. Something had to be done if she was going to help prevent illness, and soon. She wasn't a healer anymore; she was a doctor, and that was different.

"Fuck," she said aloud, with a twisted kind of relief. Things were hopeless. Her healing abilities were drying up. Anything could kill them. A common cold.

Through these thoughts, Pinot could see May's lank hair, could hear the acid in her words. Insatiable anger ran under Pinot's skin like a boiling river. She let herself succumb to it, just for a little while.

Brittni Brinn

Chapter 7
Arissa

Arissa kept her mittened hands deep in her pockets as the wind brushed against her padded coat. Lazy snowflakes mingled with the yellow leaves fluttering to the ground in front of her. The cloud cover was patchy enough to allow glimpses of the crisp morning sky. She closed her eyes, breathing in deeply through her nose, out through her mouth. Her breath faded into the fabric of the forest.

She headed around the restaurant, following the reddish dirt path that years of walkers had worn into the earth. The finishing glaze on the restaurant's exterior was showing signs of wear: come spring, they'd have to reseal the log wall, replace some of the shingles. All they could do for now was keep the flue clear and hope it would hold together through another winter.

She turned her eyes to the mostly bare trees, scatterings of auburn and crimson showing through the mint and navy strains of evergreen. The woods extended back for an acre before dropping off. If she wanted, she could look down and find the edge miles away where the tree line stopped and the earth turned flat and barren. For today, Arissa kept to the middle of the acre, encompassed entirely by forest.

It was a welcome break. Usually, the clamor of faces and intentions she was sensitive to would perforate her consciousness. It used to be so acute, she could wake up in the middle of the night and know exactly who was having nightmares and who was in the middle of a pleasant dream. Now it was more of a murky river; she had to strain to see beyond what the person across from her was presenting to the world.

Even now, she felt someone coming down from the restaurant, but wasn't sure it was Theodore until he appeared on the edge of her vision.

"Morning," she smiled up at her nephew. It was hard to believe how much he'd grown in the past couple of years. His sleeves were rolled up into loose cuffs over his bare hands. The jacket, an old coat of his dad's, was too big for him, but she knew he didn't mind: he found loose clothes more comfortable.

Theodore shyly held out a crabapple.

"Did you bring this for me?" she asked.

"Yes," he affirmed in his quiet, strained voice.

"But what about you?" she said, "Did you have breakfast yet?"

Theodore, still offering the crabapple, extended his other hand. It was empty. He held it face up, keeping his palms parallel. Arissa blinked, and as she did, another apple, identical to the first, appeared on the surface of his empty palm.

They ate the apples together, listening as the birds began to call to each other to keep warm.

***

Arissa had just hung her coat on the back of the kitchen door and was about to change her boots for her moccasins, when May walked into the dining hall. Her shoulders drooped as she carried Lucas through the empty tables. Arissa turned on the kettle, which someone had already filled with water the night before. Instead of collecting rain in barrels or hiking down the gentler side of the hill to the stream, they'd soon be melting snow. At least the camping generator was back online. It usually needed an occasional kick start from Ed, but last week it had stopped running altogether. Thank God they'd got it working.

Ulway (he hated being called Theodore she reminded

herself) had been integral in that of course. Once their resident engineer, Victoria, found the cause of the problem, her nephew had disappeared with the part in question and returned with a perfect copy. People at the restaurant thought he was very good at fixing things, but it was more than that. She could still taste the sour sweetness of the crabapple he'd given her before eating his own. When she was able to get one box of pasta from a trade caravan, Ulway would keep a handful in a jar and duplicate it as many times as they needed. His ability was incredible. It was the only thing keeping them alive in the winter.

But if her ability was starting to falter, did that mean Ulway's would follow close behind?

Arissa stirred a spoonful of instant coffee into a mug of hot water as she pushed the kitchen door open with her back. The dining room was washed in clear grey light from the bank of windows along the far wall. May had settled into one of the padded chairs near the empty fireplace, one arm propped on the table, the other holding Lucas, who was finally asleep. Arissa set the mug of coffee within her reach and took the seat across from her. An unlit candle sat between them.

"It wasn't a good night." May stared at the ashes scattering the stone mantle.

"I gathered. Drink some of that."

May shifted her son as she reached for the coffee. He made a small noise before settling back into sleep. She sighed in relief and picked up the mug. Studying the chipped white porcelain, she sighed again. She set the mug on the table and looked Arissa straight in the eyes. They sat there a moment, perfectly still.

May shook her head. "How are you doing? I can't tell at all."

"It's disturbing, isn't it?"

"Last year, I could tell it was starting to go. But now, I can be at home with Isak and the baby, and I can't hear their emotions at all. It used to be a kind of constant soundtrack, but now there's only silence." She glanced over at the woods through the back bay of windows. "Still, even if it is different, it's kind of nice. No more of people's emotional baggage to wade through every time I enter a room. Except—"

Arissa waited for May to turn back to her. "Except what?"

May shook her head again, which jostled Lucas just enough to wake him up. It was sudden, and the room was strange and he was hungry. May *shhed* to try and calm him, directing a wry smile at Arissa. "When I say silence, I only mean in the figurative sense, of course."

"It's alright." Arissa stood up and tucked her chair beneath the table. "It's time for me to set out breakfast anyway. We'll have plenty of time to talk later."

"It's nice to be back."

Arissa warmly rubbed May's shoulder and headed to the kitchen. Twenty minutes later, as she arranged the coffee things for the early risers, she noted that May was in the same chair, breastfeeding the baby under an old green and blue quilt.

Pinot staggered up the stairs, her loose hair hanging over her sharp cheeks. Arissa poured a mug of coffee for her, setting the honey close by. As Pinot reached the counter, May tensed forward, her expression alert. Stirring her coffee, Pinot gave Arissa a mumbled thanks before heading down the hallway to the clinic. May watched her go, not relaxing even after it was clear that Pinot was not coming back.

Arissa studied the scene a few moments longer. May finally turned away from the hallway. She adjusted her shirt, removed the quilt and kissed her son's head. Arissa sensed a stab of something like fear from May, the clearest sign she had felt for weeks.

"Silence...except—" Arissa said to herself as the clinic door closed behind Pinot. "Except..."

Chapter 8
A Game

Sophie and Milo decided to play cards.

"Canasta's no fun with two," he'd said, but they were playing anyway. Sophie was already in her second hand and he still needed another red row to go out. She placed a black three in the discard, freezing the pile.

"Your go," she set her cards face down on the wood-grained table.

"Where'd you get the cards, Sophie?" he casually asked as he tried to strategize a way through his first hand. The two cards he picked up from the deck were of no help. He sadly discarded a red four, knowing that he'd be lucky to get another turn.

"Oh, we were a card playing family, my brothers and me. I always carry a deck of cards in my purse." She laid a row of eights aside. "You never know when you'll need them." A joker on a row made another little pile of cards, this time with a black queen on top. Sophie discarded her remaining ten of hearts and clapped her hands. "I'm out!"

"You win." Milo started to get up from the table.

"No, no, no, you get back here," she said, making a pushing motion with her small wrinkled hand. "We have to count up our points."

Milo sat down, not unwillingly. It felt better to have his back supported, to be grounded in the chair. Getting up sometimes brought with it a wave of vertigo and lightheadedness. And then the jabbing in his bladder would start up and he would have to pee, painfully, barely avoiding passing out.

"I clearly lost this one," he tried to persuade her. She insisted, counting up his points by tapping her blunt fingernails on the table. She cleared his score by almost 2000 points but seemed surprised that she had won.

"You're not very good at winning," she said, "but you're a sporting opponent."

"Thank you," Milo replied, something small coming to his attention. He'd tried to convince her not to worry about the score, and she had ignored his request. Could she resist his persuasive efforts? He decided to try again, focusing his ability so that his consciousness seemed to collect into a single point directed at the elderly woman across from him. "Better pack up and have a nap now, Sophie."

She burst out with a croaking laugh. "I may be old, but I'm no quitter. No, no, young man, I'm going to give you a chance to make this even." And she started shuffling the cards, expertly flipping the two halves of the deck into each other and then tapping the edges square.

Milo couldn't believe it. "Sophie, don't shuffle the cards."

She shuffled the deck twice more and then dealt. "You can go first this time," she said and the game began.

Chapter 9
Tears

Pinot was trying to squeeze a tear from her eye into a small glass bottle when Ed appeared in the clinic doorway.

"Dammit." The one tear she had coaxed out of herself splattered useless on the floor.

Ed stood motionless, one hand on either side of the frame.

"Come in if you're coming," Pinot said, her jaw tight. Instead of propelling the bottle to follow her wasted tear, she placed it firmly on the counter.

He came in and sat on the bench.

"Looks like you've been through hell." Pinot didn't even try at professionalism with Ed. They knew each other too well for that.

He rolled his eyes.

"What?" Pinot leaned back against the counter. "You're here to see the doctor, aren't you? Tell me what's wrong."

Ed shook his head.

"You won't tell me what's wrong?"

Ed rolled his eyes again.

"You… didn't come to see the doctor."

A sarcastic thumbs up.

"You came to see me."

He nodded and wrote something on the pad of paper he carried around with him. He handed it to Pinot.

"Oh."

Ed patted the seat next to him.

"I'm fine, Ed."

He gave her a look, the one she knew meant in all seriousness that he did not believe her bullshit.

It was her turn to roll her eyes, but she sat down anyway. She handed him back his notepad.

You're angry, he wrote.

Even now, she was grasping the handle of her switchblade. "Yes."

I thought you and May talked about it. Followed by a giant question mark.

"Sure we did. Then they went to live in that little cabin and I thought I could ignore them until I left."

Until you left?

"Shit. I didn't mean—"

He thrust the paper in front of her eyes, cutting off the rest of her excuse. *You're leaving?*

"No, no, I'm not. Not for a while, anyway."

What the hell, Pinot!

"Just, I don't think it's a good idea for me to stay here."

What are you talking about?

"It's just not a good idea!" she repeated, the bubbling anger rising into her throat.

I feel just as out of place here as you.

"Oh, so this is about you, now?"

Nobody really talks to me. Just you, Arissa, and now Milo and Rhonda. I'm just the power guy.

"Maybe if you didn't sleep with everything that moved, you'd find it easier to make friends."

Fucking hypocrite.

Ed waited until she had read it and then tore the whole book of paper in half.

Pinot let the surface break, feeling some long-forgotten personal idiom brewing in her mouth. "You're a sullied piece of poser," she relished telling him. "Get out."

He left the clinic shaking his head. She listened to his shallow breathing fade down the hall.

Pinot had no trouble filling the rest of the bottle, and by lights-on had figured out a way to infuse her tears into a solution that could be injected or swallowed.

Brittni Brinn

Chapter 10
Ed

Ed didn't think he'd slept with *that* many people. Maybe half a dozen in the four years he'd been here, and that was nothing compared to his pre-Event exploits. None of his relationships here had been one-night stands. One relationship had only lasted a week—she'd taken up with a trading caravan, hoping to track down her brother. Justin had been about a month, and they'd parted on friendly terms. Ed's longest relationship had been with Joyce. She'd been seven years older than him and enjoyed role playing. They'd spent most of their nights in the cramped storage room upstairs weaving stories and their bodies around each other. But she got tired of him, and after their last big fight had run off with a Grafter who'd stumbled on the restaurant while looking for supplies.

Only one of his exes was still living in the restaurant. Victoria. She'd been an engineer before the Event and now helped Arissa with upkeep of the building, especially the well. The remote restaurant had been built nearly 50 years ago, so it had its own well, which meant that the building still enjoyed the benefit of working toilets. Ed provided power, but when something structural came apart, Victoria was the person who ended up fixing it. He'd admired that about her—he still did. They shared some interests, but after a few dates—if any activity in the constant public space of the restaurant could be called a date—they'd agreed that they weren't compatible and had emotionally parted ways.

Fuck you, Pinot, Ed thought at last, this time able to feel vindicated. She couldn't blame his loneliness on a handful of relationships. If he wanted to, he could throw her argument right back in her face. Everyone knew that she and Nick snuck off together. But it wasn't worth it.

He clicked out of the programming window he'd been working on, and opened the brand-new level of *Trace of Shadows*, drumming his fingertips on his desk as it loaded. Rhonda had called the game an RPG, but it wasn't one, not really. Ed was writing an IF, a text-based adventure game. He couldn't quite kick his need to have a visual element, though, and liked the simple grid and sprite he'd developed. He'd been on the designing board for many video games in his career before the Event; now he regretted not paying more attention to the actual programming process.

Onscreen, a blocky approximation of a human appeared in the center of the grid. He moved it three squares to the right and let the encounter load.

A dark blue banner spanned the bottom of the screen, framing a section of white text:

You are faced with a metal case mounted on the wall. The top is latched but unlocked.

He typed OPEN CASE into the command bar and tapped the Enter key.

As you open the lid, a small lizard, blazing orange and green, bursts out and jumps onto the wall.

He typed in X LIZARD.

You catch the lizard in your hands. Even through your thick leather gloves, you can feel heat emanating from the lizard.

He typed in TAKE LIZARD.

You put the lizard in your pouch.

Ed typed WALK SOUTH.

The original grid appeared, his sprite now sporting a small flame on its shoulder. He progressed down five squares. Another text box loaded:

A woman in a white dress appears in front of you. She is incredibly beautiful.

GIVE LIZARD TO WOMAN.

The woman takes the lizard from you and catches on fire. She reveals her true form, a dungeon wraith.

Without hesitation, Ed typed KISS DUNGEON WRAITH and hit Enter.

The text box exploded (a pixelated mess he was extremely proud of) revealing a glowing line of text:

THE DUNGEON WRAITH HAS JOINED YOUR PARTY.

Brittni Brinn

Chapter 11
Bedside Manner

1. Greet your patient by name.
2. Offer them a seat if they are not already comfortable.
3. Start off the conversation by asking a question.
4. Keep your tone friendly and professional. Smile.
5. Practice active listening. Maintain eye contact.
6. Acknowledge their concerns.
7. Offer appropriate treatment or explain available options.
8. You may choose to show empathy by placing a hand on your patient's shoulder.

A steady knock on the clinic door brought Pinot out of the page she was reading. Milo waited in the doorway, trying to keep the pain out of his face.

"Hey, Milo." Pinot let the textbook fall closed and tossed it lightly onto the counter. "Have a seat."

Milo chose the sturdy plastic chair. Pinot shut the door and sat facing him on the padded bench. "How are you feeling today?"

"A little groggy."

Pinot nodded, maintaining eye contact. "How've you been sleeping?" Her tone friendly, professional.

"Not great, to be honest. I'm not used to sleeping in a room with so many other people. And besides," he leaned a bit closer, his voice taking on an overdramatic whisper. "Markus snores."

Pinot smiled, a slight lifting of the corners of her mouth. "Not much I can do about that. But there're some herbal teas in the kitchen you can try…"

"It's getting worse." Milo's jaw worked, the humor of his last comment completely absent. His eyes moved to meet hers and then lowered to study his clasped hands.

There wasn't much more Pinot could say. In the handful of days Milo had been at the restaurant, he'd lost his appetite along with about five pounds. His watch hung loosely from his wrist. His cheeks sagged, the wrinkles carved deep around his mouth and eyes. His movements were slow and minimal, as if to stave off the pain that could strike at any moment. It was definitely getting worse.

Pinot knew that a hand on the shoulder would be appropriate, but she couldn't bring herself to move. She didn't feel any sense of empathy, only emptiness. Instead, she said "I'll do everything I can," wondering if that was anything at all.

Chapter 12
Hidden Camera

Rhonda concealed her camera underneath her windbreaker. Even though she and Milo had been at the restaurant for a couple weeks, she still didn't trust the place— the fewer people who knew she had a camera, the better. Usually, she kept it bundled at the bottom of her backpack, crammed in the space between the cot mattress and the metal bar that made up the foot of her bed, covered over with the folded wool blanket. A shoddy hiding place considering her camera's previous cache in the wall. Why'd we have to leave? she inwardly raved. But of course, she already knew why.

She threw the thought away and focused instead on what she would be filming. A ridge on the side of the hill just behind the restaurant. The view of the wasteland from there was incredible, and Rhonda was drawn to it in a way that left no room for doubt. She had to film it.

Cradling the camera under her jacket in case the strap around her neck slipped, Rhonda left the bedroom. She made it to the top of the stairs without running into anyone. The dining hall was clear, except for May and her baby, sitting on the far side of the room. Rhonda almost took out her camera to take a short recording of the afternoon sunlight catching in the window and highlighting her profile, her baby asleep in her arms. But Milo was coming down the hall from the clinic, she recognized his steady footsteps. She was about to move to meet him when Nick came in from the foyer, his face red from running.

"Hi Rhonda!" he called, passing his sweater sleeve over his forehead.

"Oh, hey."

He came right up to her, stretching his arms across his chest. "How're you settling in?"

Rhonda tried to smile back, but was nervous. What did he want? "Okay. Everyone's been really nice."

"Yeah, it's a good group here. Who've you met so far?"

"Pinot, of course. Arissa, Theo—Ulway, I mean. Ed."

"Have you tried his game yet?" Nick asked her, running a hand through his glossy blond hair.

"Nah," Rhonda held the camera close under her jacket. "It's good?"

Nick shrugged. "Passes the time. I'm not that good at it, but Sophie I've heard can get all the way to the third dungeon."

"Sophie? Like, that 90-year-old lady?"

He nodded, smiling in a way Rhonda felt was exactly tuned to her.

"Maybe I'll try it tonight."

"Stay warm," Nick said as Milo joined them. "It's brisk out there." He beamed at them both before veering off into the dining area.

Milo was bundled up for their daily walk in the woods. "You look happy about something," he noted as he and Rhonda approached the foyer.

"Yeah," she replied. "I guess I am." She looked over her shoulder. Nick had found a clear space beyond the tables and was going through a yoga salutation. He turned his torso and caught her looking at him. He winked.

"Let's go," she squeaked out, and bee-lined for the main doors.

***

That evening, Rhonda sat in front of one of the blank computer monitors, settling in for the wait until 7pm.

"You're here!" Someone sat in the seat next to her. It was Nick, wearing a V-neck t-shirt and jeans.

"Oh, hi. I, I thought I'd try it out."

"Yeah, when you said you were interested, it got me thinking about the game. I haven't played for a few weeks. Thought it'd be worth another go."

"What's the point? Of the game, I mean. Do I have to shoot zombies, or…?"

Nick leaned back into the padded green chair, letting his bare arms laze over the wooden armrests. "Did you ever play one of those really old video games? The ones with the text boxes you had to type answers to? It's kind of like a choose-your-own-adventure. The point of the game is not to die."

The overhead lights hummed to life and the screen in front of her oozed blue. Rhonda sat up in her chair and shook the mouse, getting used to it again, the feeling of communing with a machine.

Nick leaned across and showed her how to navigate the login screen. She typed in TheRealRhonda37, followed by her password. A simple desktop appeared, featuring two icons: a white square labelled "WEEKLY MEMO" and a pixelated sword called "TRACE OF SHADOWS."

"'Weekly Memo?'"

"Yeah," Nick said, signing into his own account. "Just some announcements, the menu for the week, who's helping with what meals. Saves paper." He grinned over to her. "Ready?" He posed his cursor over the *Trace of Shadows* icon.

Rhonda did the same. "Don't die. Got it."

Brittni Brinn

Chapter 13
Wilson

A Grafter approached. Tearing down the western highway, the growl of his motorcycle engine loud enough to echo up through the trees to the acre behind the restaurant.

It was still early in the day, around mid-morning. Milo was out walking, slowly, alone. Keeping one foot in front of the other, focusing on the steady trunk of the closest tree if he started to feel lightheaded. The distant whine and canker of the engine caught his attention. Sparked a sense of familiarity, a distant memory. He remembered the carrot and the desperate cruelty in the Grafter's eyes, visible even in the dark.

"No, no...have to...warn them..." His words sounded strange to him, his tongue thick in his mouth. He turned back towards the log-walled building, but his vision started to tilt, the tree trunks crossing themselves in ghostly x-s. And long before the Grafter found the restaurant, Milo collapsed.

***

The Grafter's name was Wilson, and he'd been driving for almost three hours. The dull ache in his lower back and the numbness starting to creep up his legs swirled through his consciousness like an undercurrent, the wind on the highway rushing over him and his motorcycle like icy seas. But he couldn't give himself to it, the constant roar across his face, the smell of gasoline. The highway was cracked up and potted.

Barely holding together after five years of fallowing like a field. Nature was taking it back, heaving off the pavement and battering it with winds and precipitation. He needed all of his attention. He needed to avoid the ruts, skim over the imperfections.

He'd have to stop soon. There had been no settlements, no trading caravans. Above all, he needed supplies. Fuel. Water. A bit of food. Somewhere warm to spend the winter. Once the snows came, he'd be ice-locked.

He was familiar with the forest, but had only just learned of the settlement on the hill, a restaurant of some kind. It was off the highway, a traveler had told him, up behind the ridge. Wilson slowed as the ridge came into view, looking for the dirt road opening the treeline. A redcedar and an oak, both overgrown, kept it from view. These he had been told about as well. Trading caravans liked to keep their routes discreet, dissuade Grafters from following their tracks.

Once past the overgrown trees, the dirt road was clear, a packed down surface listing up and to the right. His motorcycle slowly climbed the incline, thick treads biting into the dirt. A log-sided building came into view, thin white smoke waterfalling across the roof. Wilson leaned back on the gas, let the bike come to a rolling stop. He disembarked, maneuvered the machine to lean on its chrome kickstand, and walked unhurriedly to the front doors. As he reached them, he heard voices coming up the side of the building. Three women were carrying what seemed to be an unconscious old man, and they had only just noticed Wilson.

"Having trouble, ladies?" Wilson grinned, his hungry eyes gleaming.

"Don't touch him!" the fattest one said, placing a protective arm over the geezer's chest.

A woman with burn marks over half of her face growled, "I'm a doctor. Let us handle this."

The oldest of the bunch, a middle-aged woman, peered into his eyes. "Once we get him inside, I can help you with whatever you need."

"Very kind, very kind," Wilson said. "Why don't I hold the door for you?"

In complete silence, the women carried the man through the door as Wilson propped it open with his foot.

He watched as they turned into a room at the end of the hall. The oldest woman was onto him, he knew. His hands were busy with a revolver, filling the empty chambers with fresh ammo.

Once he'd secured the gun in his pocket, Wilson released the door and sauntered inside, drawn into the dining room by the pretty sight of a woman holding a baby. He scanned the rest of the place. Only one person in the kitchen. And two of the three carrying-women coming back down the hallway.

"Now that that's settled." The older woman motioned to one of the tables, while the freak doctor looked on. "What can we do for you?"

"Oh," Wilson said as he drew the gun from his pocket, "I think quite a lot."

Chapter 14
Blood

The Grafter moved to the computers, allured by the plastic keys and blank screens. "These work?"

They all stood stiffly, only their eyes moving. Arissa had gathered the residents on the Grafter's request. They waited in a jumble, cornered in the far side of the dining room. Milo's groans echoed down the hallway.

"What do you want?" Arissa said in a calm and steady voice.

The Grafter looked around the room. "Whatever you've got." He pointed his gun at May, bearing down on her. "This, for instance." He held the muzzle of the gun to her chin, smiling down at Lucas as he picked him up and maneuvered him into the crook of his free arm. The Grafter kept his gun pointed at May's chest. "I want to know where you keep all of your supplies. I want everyone to bring their belongings into this room. And then, I want you all to quietly walk out into the woods, where I will shoot some of you as the rest run away. I won't chase you, I promise. As long as you leave behind everything that's mine." He gripped Lucas closer to him, sending a leering grin over to May. "If any of you so much as think of bringing a weapon back with you, you know what'll happen."

Arissa took a step forward, but the Grafter smirked. "What a healthy baby you are," he cooed to the sleeping child, "I'd hate for anything terrible to happen to you."

Arissa sighed as if defeated. "Everybody, do what he asks."

The small crowd hurried downstairs or disappeared into the kitchen. Everyone except for Pinot.

"What's up, doc?" the Grafter grinned, his gun still aimed directly at May.

Pinot shot a glance around, and seeing that everyone else was gone, took a step closer to him. "I could stay too," she said coyly, using her right hand to slowly unzip her hoodie. "These people are so fucking dull. I think you'd be fun."

The Grafter hesitated. Pinot drew closer, just out of his reach. The gun lowered. But someone was coming up the stairs. His head snapped to the right, losing sight of Pinot. Realizing his mistake, the Grafter tried raising the gun to reassert his power over May. But something was wrong. His arm wouldn't move. In fact, his whole body had gone stiff.

And that's when Pinot brought her left hand around, the blade inside burying into his temple.

The Grafter and the gun fell together. The dead man's arm crumpled harmlessly as Pinot caught Lucas and lifted him away. May rushed forward, her hands sliding around Lucas; she staggered a couple of steps, sitting heavily in one of the chairs, her son clutched to her chest.

"That was close—You— you got Lucas away—" May stopped short as Pinot knelt and wrenched the knife from the dead Grafter's head. "Pinot?"

Pinot brought the knife down again. It lodged in the dead man's stomach. She threw one leg over, straddling the corpse's thighs, cutting away his clothing. The knife came down again, opening the Grafter's wasted gut. She reached in her bare hand, and tore at the entrails, splattering her face with blood.

"Pinot!" May yelled, "What the hell are you doing? Stop it! Ed, make her stop!" Ed stood transfixed at the top of the stairs, his eyes tight, his hand gripping the banister.

It was Arissa who finally wrenched Pinot away from the corpse, dragging her outside.

"You're filthy!" Arissa screamed, throwing her at the trees.

"Go and clean yourself up!"

Pinot straightened. The Grafter's blood coated her hands, now hanging loose and empty at her sides. But her eyes were on fire, they burned with a cold greed that Arissa felt deep in her stomach.

"He deserved it, the slimy chucked up putrid mess of garbage, he was a fucking pile of feces and HE DESERVED IT."

"And you are acting like an animal!"

Pinot smirked, wiping some of the blood from her face with the cuff of her still open hoodie. Beneath it was her only t-shirt, worn black cloth with the neck cut out. "What's that? Everyone's safe now? The *baby* is safe, he's okay? Oh, you're welcome, you're so welcome."

"I had everything under control," Arissa growled, "Ed was going to enter his brain circuitry and disarm him, and then we were going to—"

"There was nothing else we could have done!" Pinot interrupted her as if she had been wanting to interrupt Arissa for a very long time. "I almost thought about not doing it. I thought that we deserved whatever the Grafter was going to do. Living in harmony, high on the hill, how happy and peaceful our society is— when all it's doing is choking us, keeping us from seeing how this all ends. This Grafter was just the beginning. You haven't been ten feet from those walls in over three years, Arissa. You have no idea what the wasteland is like now. It's crawling with shit like him. And they'll find their way here, they'll come in the night and slit our throats."

Arissa ignored her. "And what am I supposed to do with that man's body? That human body that you ripped the life out of like it was nothing?"

"You take his clothes, his boots, his bike. You bury or burn the rest. That's it." Pinot turned away from Arissa and headed into the trees.

Arissa, feeling the cold burn enter her own soul, shouted after her. "Don't come back until you've washed yourself clean from this!"

But Pinot was already gone.

Chapter 15
Bearings

Running. The trees bare now, the ground caked with their corpses. All the blood, it was tingling on her skin, tightening around her fingers as it dried. Fucking stupid. His blood could be fraught with disease, could carry any kind of infection, STI, virus. Would her healing powers still work on herself? Could she trust her own blood to sieve out the enemy, to keep her from annihilation?

Pinot slowed down to get her bearings. Finding that she'd strayed too far east, she adjusted her course, walking slowly towards the stream. The cut on the back of her hand had healed over just yesterday. She could make out the raised line of new skin through the black-red all over her hands. She would be okay. It would take a couple of days, but she would be okay.

The stream tumbled over a small ridge of stones into a wide bed lined with thin ice. Pinot followed it downstream a few metres, so the blood wouldn't damage their water supply. The last thing she needed was an outbreak.

Her thoughts slowed down, her heart beating violently under her shirt. She was going to be in shock, she noted, kneeling next to the stream and washing her hands in the painfully cold water. She grabbed some leaves from the ground next to her and scrubbed at the blood splattering her arms all the way up to her elbows. She applied a few icy splashes to her face. Her clothes desperately needed a wash, but that could wait for the evening. She could heat up some water and use the industrial detergent from the kitchen to get the stains out. Or she could burn them.

Pinot took deep breaths, sitting back on the stream bank and sticking her arms into the warmth of the soiled hoodie. She counted to 100, a trick she'd learned from an old cures and ailments dictionary. She waited another minute or so before pushing herself up and walking back towards the restaurant. Only now did she fully register how cold it was, her breath billowing up in front of her.

She slipped into the warm interior of the restaurant. The corpse was gone. Sophie was instructing Stef and Markus as they scrubbed the blood stains out of the floor. Back near the fireplace, Nick was talking with Rhonda. Pinot watched as Nick drew her into a full and long embrace. With the last bit of energy remaining to her, Pinot turned and walked down the hallway. I'm not even angry, she thought absently, just tired.

Arissa met her at the clinic door. "All washed. Good. Milo needs your full attention."

"Milo, shit," Pinot remembered. "Is he okay?" But she could see that he wasn't. "Looks like exposure," she said, her voice feeling far away, "and I'm going to need some gauze for that cut." And just like that, she was back into it.

But something had changed, unmistakably and forever. It wasn't just the Grafter, not just the blood, or Arissa, or the restaurant. It was something inside of her. Something new, but also familiar. And she knew, at that moment, that she couldn't stay here, not for one more fucking day.

Chapter 16
Leaving

An LED lamp sat on the nightstand next to Ed, casting sharp shadows over the sheets. He was sitting on her bed, waiting for her.

Pinot sat on the opposite end, rearranging the long-knitted sweater over the skirt Arissa had lent her while her clothes dried. "What do you want?" She kept her voice low, aware of the sleeping residents in the room's five other beds.

Ed shrugged, then made the motion of pulling out his intestines. He shrugged again.

"Yeah, I guess I overdid it."

His face and body laughed at her understatement. She couldn't help but join him, her pent-up adrenaline using her quiet laughter as an outlet. Once their breath ran out, they sat together in silence.

"You broke your promise," Pinot whispered.

Ed nodded, hands gripping his knees.

"Guess you kind of had to do it. The Grafter had Lucas, you couldn't just let things play out." Pinot moved to sit next to him. "Must've been weird, being all up in someone else's brain after so many years."

He turned to her, frowning.

"Oh, I didn't mean it like that. We're good. I don't blame you for... for what you did to Jax."

Ed sighed, soundlessly. He pulled a piece of paper from his pocket and penned a few words onto it. He angled the message so Pinot could make out his shaky handwriting in the dim light.

You blame May.

"She made you do it, you know that as well as I do. Manipulated you so you'd control him, short circuit his brain with your electricity thing—Jax wasn't going to hurt me, he—" Pinot cut herself off, seething. "Good thing he got out when he did."

Ed scrawled something else and handed it to her.

Don't go.

"But I'm already packed," Pinot lied. That would be for the early morning. Changing into her dried clothes, stealing supplies from the clinic and the kitchen. She'd already written up a list of what everybody had and how to treat them to leave for Arissa. "I have to," she told him, an edge in her voice.

This place needs you, he wrote next.

She scoffed.

Then: *I'm coming too.*

"Like hell you are."

Ed shook his head, but Pinot interrupted. "You have a life here. You said you don't fit in, but it suits you. You're making video games, like before the Event, isn't that what you wanted? You have relative security, and supplies, and people who care about you—"

Ed shook his head again. *It's not what I wanted.*

"Then what do you want?"

Dunno. He handed her the paper and shrugged.

Pinot tried to make out his features in the LED shadows. His cheeks were so drawn in, they looked like dark caves, his eyes glittered in shallow recesses of their own. The hair over his forehead twined like marble rivulets.

"You're sure." It was an acknowledgement. "Travelling the wasteland, together, after so long. It'll be different, this time." She reached across him to shut off the light. "No one telling us where to go. We get to choose."

Ed got up to leave, but Pinot caught his hand. "You don't have to." She shuffled over to make room for him and they fell asleep for a few short hours, their sweatered shoulders touching in the dark.

Brittni Brinn

Chapter 17
Layers

Arissa could peel back the layers of people's thoughts. Most layers were paper-thin, they came free easily, like removing a sticky note. The under-layers, those could be more difficult, like peeling band-aids. And after a while, if she went far enough, the layers were superglued and couldn't be removed at all. It was how she could tell if people were hiding something. How she'd known that May and Ed and Pinot would be safe additions to the restaurant all those years ago. Now, it was as if she was wearing oven mitts and could only manage to grasp one layer between her bulky thumb and conglomerate of fingers.

One layer was all she'd needed last night. She'd seen Pinot's face beneath the facade: determined, someone who was set on their course. Pinot was tending to Milo, but underneath the decision was made. She would leave.

Arissa splayed her hands on either side of the list Pinot had left behind, the names of each resident and their hidden conditions. Stef was having severe stomach cramps and needed to take a dose of apple cider every couple of days. *Parasite* was circled with a question mark next to her name. Sophie was vulnerable to bronchial infection. Nick had *Rotten molar* next to his name, underlined. *Rinse mouth out daily with saltwater.* Beside Milo's name, *Bladder cancer.*

Arissa sighed. There wasn't much any of them could do.

Pinot had left instructions on how to use the small bottle of tears in teas or bandages, but even Arissa was aware of how little it would accomplish. Pinot's abilities were starting to fade, just like her own.

This is unacceptable, Arissa thought to herself. How could Pinot leave her patients this way? The girl didn't realize it was her presence as much as her ability that helped people. And Ed had left with her. Arissa was not looking forward to telling everyone that the lights wouldn't be coming on that evening. Once again, they'd have to adapt, get used to living without.

Arissa folded the patient list and secured it in the pocket of her grey knit sweater. Two people she had trusted: gone. It was the nature of things, she forced herself to accept the stoic truth of it. People came. People went.

Chapter 18
Take Care

Milo slid his watch up onto his wrist as Rhonda sat on the chair at the side of his bed. "They told me she ran off," he responded to her charged silence.

"Yeah."

Milo exhaled through his nose, folding his wasted hands over the blanket. "She left me some pills."

"Oh fucking good for her."

"Rhonda."

"This whole thing was a waste of time. We could've just stayed home."

"Rhonda."

"Don't."

"These are good people. They'll take care of you when—"

"These people?" she scoffed. "These are good? Would good people abandon you?"

Milo shook his head. "That Grafter wasn't good."

Rhonda looked sideways at him, taken off-guard. "Obviously."

"I'd seen him before."

Rhonda paused, then spoke even louder, folding her arms. "Oh yeah?"

"He came to the school."

"No he didn't. I would've seen."

"In the middle of the night. I used to stay up and watch out for Grafters. There were a few over the years."

"I told them off, too. All by myself while you were inside. They didn't come back."

Milo shook his head again. "They did, in the middle of the night, ready to kill us or worse."

Rhonda was speechless for a moment. "Did you kill them, Milo?"

He laughed. "Of course not."

"Then...what did you do?"

He motioned her to lean closer. "I've heard stories about Pinot since we got here. She used to heal people just by spitting on their injuries. And you know how Ed can control electricity?"

"The Event changed them," Rhonda said, recalling Pinot's earlier explanation.

Milo raised his eyebrows as if sharing in a secret joke. "It changed something about me too."

"What?"

"I can convince people to do something they don't want to do. I can persuade them to go a different way, to choose a different outcome. So when that Grafter came while you were sleeping, I told him I was a poor old man and that there was nothing worth taking from me. I sent him off after the trading caravan instead, knowing they were well-protected. I suppose he never caught up to them, or was drawn off that path somehow."

Rhonda suddenly stood, her voice pitching with anger. "That's how you got me to come here with you. You used your powers on me!"

"My powers? Haha—," Milo grimaced a little and finished the laugh. "It's not magic, I don't think. Just an enhancement. I did persuade you. But it was the right thing to do. If you had stayed, I wouldn't have been there to look after you. Rhonda," his voice grew quiet, "you're like a daughter to me, you really are. I wish my own daughters could've had the chance to meet you. So please, don't be angry." He sighed. "You don't owe me anything. But... I want you to stay here with these people, make a life for yourself, and be happy. You wouldn't have been happy if you had stayed at the school. But you can be here."

Rhonda glared at him, and then left the room, slamming the wooden door behind her.

Milo settled back into his pillow. "Well." He closed his eyes, another sigh gathering in his lungs. "Going to take some time."

Brittni Brinn

Chapter 19
Flashback

Watching the candlelight flicker on the blank infirmary wall, Arissa thought back to the night she met May and Pinot. The middle of a deep sleepless night, almost a year after the Event. Arissa had been pacing the storage room, perching occasionally on the edge of her camping cot. Maybe she was thinking of her sister Carey, hoping that she and Malcom had survived. Or maybe she was worrying about Theodore, how he was still missing his parents in his quiet way. How long would they have to wait until they had to let go? She didn't want to consider it.

That's when she'd heard someone yelling outside, pounding on the door. Her nephew came into her room, and although she couldn't see his face in the dim candlelight, she could see the uncertainty in him. The desperate hope that his parents were beyond the heavy front door, despite the many disappointments he'd already gone through.

Leading him into the kitchen, Arissa told him to wait until she had sounded out whoever was knocking. She left the candle on one of the empty round tables.

"I'm looking for my husband!" someone called through the door. The voice said her name was May.

Arissa retreated into the shadows as the person beyond entered. She sensed May's presence and peeled back the first layer.

May was breathing hard from her trip up the hill, not to mention the effort she had put into getting into the restaurant. The woman was curious, searching, but there was no malice that Arissa could sense.

"Hello?" May said, her voice spinning up through the rafters and glancing off the bare wooden tables.

Arissa picked up the candle and approached, her moccasins making no sound on the old laminate. "Welcome," Arissa said, "Welcome to our refuge."

May was looking for Isak, who had jumped ahead in time. A gift Arissa had never considered possible, even with the evidence of her and Theodore's new abilities. But Arissa was more concerned with the next layer of May. Underneath her need to find Isak was something disturbing. A grimace, laced with guilt. Ashamed.

"Tell me what you've done," Arissa said after she'd invited May to sit down. Her hand set the candle between them, her movements gentle, accepting. To do anything else would close the conversation. The layer had been so easy to peel back. This woman wanted to tell someone. Wanted someone to notice.

So many layers beneath, pressed down or ignored. Buried in order to survive. May flipped through them concisely: the tension between loneliness and community, the stress of holding her group together, her misguided attempt to protect Pinot.

(Oh Pinot, Arissa couldn't help but think as she listened for Milo's hollow breathing. Where are you now?)

That night— it had all started there for May and Pinot. Once Jax found out about May and Ed's efforts to manipulate him, he'd stormed out, leaving Ed in a puddle of blood, leaving Pinot with the marred remnant of their relationship, leaving May with her guilt.

After everything that happened, the clearest image Arissa had of that night was of May facing the window, wringing her hands as Jax ran further and further into the forest. Following his pain until he was out of her reach.

"You're deep in thought," Milo noted.

Arissa left the image and returned to her seat next to his bed. "I thought you were asleep."

Milo shifted on the bed so he could face her. "Well, I'm awake now," he said, his eyes untouched by the usual pain. "What were you thinking about?"

"May."

"The person or the month of?"

Arissa smiled. "I think you know."

"You've known each other for a long time."

"Four years, give or take a few months. I was happy when she came to live here. I was happy when they all decided to stay. But the rift between May and Pinot. I always regretted not doing more."

"What happened between them?"

Arissa straightened in her seat, the subject pushing her into alertness. "It's not just one thing. Well, it started with one thing. May used to be able to change how people feel, to tweak their emotional responses. She was worried about a Grafter who was holding them hostage. She used her ability to make Ed control the Grafter."

"They were prisoners?"

"Essentially. Jax, the Grafter, he'd taken their supplies and forced them all to come with him and his group as they moved west."

"Wait, who was forced? Arissa, you're not telling this very well," Milo teased.

"Ed, Pinot, May, and Isak. The four of them ended up together at a convenience store that survived the Event. Jax ran across them, him and his group of 20 or so. I never saw them, but May tells me that they travelled inside huge mechanical shells, some kind of experimental survival units."

Milo chuckled. "Sounds like something out of a sci-fi movie."

She shrugged, "It was how May described them."

"Keep going," Milo said suddenly, his eyes focusing on the far corner of the room as his pain started to resurface. "What happened after Jax took their supplies?"

"May and Isak were worried about Pinot." Arissa reached for the readied bowl on the floor next to her, using a washcloth to cool his forehead. "Jax had a grudge against a gang Pinot used to be a part of. They were afraid Jax would snap and decide to kill her, to get revenge."

"So May got Ed to use his power to control Jax's brain?"

"Ed would bring Jax closer to Pinot, make him turn his head, or reach for her in a crowd. Little things like that. Just to make Jax think he was interested in her. But then, it worked."

"They fell in love."

Arissa replaced the washcloth in the bowl. "Something like that."

Milo's face clouded. "She's been through a lot."

"We all have," Arissa said, helping him to shift into a more comfortable position. He groaned a little as his back settled into the thin mattress. "Do you need anything?"

Milo closed his eyes in gentle refusal. "You don't have to stay up all night for me. I'll be just fine."

She weighed this, then nodded. "Try to get some rest. I'll check on you first thing in the morning."

"Arissa," Milo reached for her shoulders as she draped the grey blanket over him. "Thank you. For me, and Rhonda. It makes it a lot easier, knowing that she has a home here."

"Of course."

They smiled at each other for a moment. Milo's eyes drooped closed, and Arissa picked up the bowl of water. She took the candle with her as she passed out of the room, leaving everything behind her in darkness.

Book Three

Book Three

Chapter 1
In the Wasteland

They both wore a backpack, each as full as they could manage. Full of food, mostly, with a change of clothes, and a couple of items they couldn't bear to leave behind.

Ed had a USB tucked into one of his pants pockets. The drive was filled with digital transpositions of five years' worth of personal journals and the storyline for *Trace of Shadows*. He'd written the originals on receipt paper, crumpled napkins, spare lined pages from the backs of old phone books. Arissa already had most of his work sealed in plastic sandwich bags, part of the archive she was collecting. She'd thought it was important to chronicle these first years after the Event, and Ed had agreed. But not before he'd typed everything out for himself. One day, he'd look back at them and remember what it was like to live alone, stranded in a convenience store, the place that had been his home for his first few months in the wasteland. So he could remember meeting May and Isak and Pinot, how Jax and his colony of SUs had carried them west. How finding Arissa had meant a new life for him.

After nearly four years, he was in the wasteland again. He walked next to Pinot. Her hard frown had returned, determination radiating from her; her stride had regained some of its lost confidence. It made him hopeful. He had lost something of himself, but here was a glimpse that he could find it again.

Pinot was thinking about her battered copy of *The Catcher in the Rye*, the only non-essential she had brought, against her better judgement. The book technically belonged to May. But it felt like hers. No one else had thumbed the pages like her, no one else had sketched out the empty-eyed adolescent on the blank cover. Even though it wore Holden's iconic hat, the face beneath was hers. Buried under packages of beef jerky, cans of peas, and sealed water bottles, a constant reminder of who she used to be.

She hunched down into the padded coat she'd nicked from behind the kitchen door on her way out. The wind was cold, and already she was imagining her tough twin mattress, climbing under the thick woolen blanket, letting it white out her mind and put her to sleep. But the blanket also brought Nick with it, and she felt his lips on her neck. You fucking hypocrite, she hissed to herself. You didn't even say goodbye.

Pinot and Ed carried their worlds on their backs, moving heavily through the wasteland like two turtles crawling across the cosmos. They walked in silence, aware of the treeline falling further and further behind them, not willing to turn back for a last auburn look. They'd had two days of picking their way through the bare trees to prepare themselves for what was coming: the long stretch of copper and tan, pockmarked by years of rain and sleet and snow, grattaged by restless winds. Ed pointed out the faintest trace of animal tracks. They followed them to a rabbit carcass, its flesh picked clean to the delicate bones.

They paused as Pinot stopped to pull at a nylon cord around her neck, fishing a compass from under her clothes. Ed took a drink from a newly opened water bottle.

"Here," Pinot cleared her throat. "I haven't treated that one yet."

Ed handed her the bottle. She spit into the dime-wide opening, swirling it before holding it out for Ed. He made a disgusted face and then grinned as he took another full sip, capping it.

"You're welcome," Pinot said, returning to the compass. It was a clear plastic square with a red arrow set inside, a dial of black dashes dividing directions. She knew that they had a day to go until the next water source, a small spring to the southwest.

Ed crouched down to study the rabbit skeleton.

"Just a bit further," she told him, and his eyes acknowledged it. The wasteland made them more gray than blue, and his expression was alert, almost cheerful. "Are you sure this is what you want?"

Ed scratched a note and he stood up, handing the paper to her.

Best I've felt in a long time.

Pinot took a quick inventory of him: the red around his eyes, the strain in his face, they were disappearing. His shoulders were starting to lift, his constant stubble filling out into a beard. His breathing, which had concerned her with its irregularity at the restaurant, was steady.

"I'm glad," she said, surprised at how much she meant it.

Pinot tucked the compass back inside her hoodie and adjusted their course. As she passed the rabbit's cracked skull, she couldn't help but notice that its empty eye sockets gaped in the direction they were going, at whatever was ahead.

Brittni Brinn

Chapter 2
Remembering
the Rules

She should have expected this. A man stood guard over the path down to the spring, a shotgun cradled in his arms. Another man leaned over an overturned plastic barrel, smiling predatorily at them. This water source had been little known to most travelers just months ago. But when Grafters found something they liked, they tended to keep a firm hold on it.

"You'll have to pay," the man behind the barrel called to them. Ed stood next to Pinot with their empty water bottles stacked in his arms. They needed this water if they were going to make it to the next settlement.

"Fine!" Pinot nodded to Ed, and he smiled just a little, encouraging her.

They set their bottles in front of the man. He was pale, his brown hair long and greasy under the black toque he wore. His breath made short clouds over his eyes whenever he wheezed. Bronchitis, Pinot thought. This man would be lucky to make it through the winter.

"Six bottles' worth, Quinten," he called behind him, and a teenager with a sour expression appeared from behind the blue tarp separating them from the spring. "If they can pay."

Pinot frowned at the man with the gun. "I have some food, if you're interested."

"What kind of food," the greasy Grafter deadpanned. "Let

me see it."

She pulled two sticks of jerky and a can of peas out from her pack for their inspection.

"That'll get you three bottles," the man appraised. "Unless you have something else for me."

"Three will be enough," Pinot said, cringing. She could see something unpleasant in the man. She didn't need Arissa's ability to read motives to know what this one was after.

"Quinten," the greasy man called back, "fill four bottles for the thirsty travelers. We'll keep the extra two."

Ed gritted his teeth, but there was nothing else to be done. The man with the gun stood by, buffing the stock with his filthy sleeve.

The teenager reappeared, two capped bottles in each hand. He placed them on top of the barrel without raising his eyes, and retreated to his place behind the tarp.

"Thank you," Pinot said as Ed gathered the bottles. They turned to go.

"We'll see you next time," the greasy man wheezed, as if he was running a family restaurant and not an exploitive tollbooth.

"Next time we come through," Pinot called back with a short wave. It was a game they were playing, and Pinot could feel herself remembering the rules. She'd gone soft sitting in that clinic day after day. If she and Ed were going to survive, she'd have to keep her senses sharp. Her switchblade was folded up in the pocket of her hoodie, a whole layer in. She unzipped the padded coat and found the familiar handle.

Ed put a water bottle in each of the wide square pockets on the front of his canvas jacket. It was the same one he'd worn years ago, when Pinot had woken up from her severe injuries and seen him for the first time. He was younger then, his red-orange hair full and wild around his face, no shallow breathing. She braced herself as a wave of hatred passed through her: *May*. That woman's schemes had run him into the ground, and his body had never recovered.

Ed took her sudden stop as an opportunity to hand her the

rest of the water bottles.

"Thanks," she said, surfacing.

He held up two fingers, pointing back to the valley they'd climbed out of.

Pinot shrugged in response. "He had a gun. No choice. Keeping two bottles is their way of intimidating us. To show us how powerless we are." One by one, she uncapped their bottles. Spit. Shook. "Anyone following us?"

Ed took stock of the wasteland behind her and shook his head.

"Good." Pinot returned each of his bottles, placed two in her backpack. "Let's keep going. I don't want to stay around here too long."

Their bearing was due west, towards the Summerland settlement. Ed handed her a note as they walked.

I wouldn't have let him shoot us.

Pinot grasped his meaning, as dangerous as the hilt of her switchblade. "I thought you wanted to keep that promise."

That promise. Ed had almost died making it.

He nodded, but his eyebrows pressed down.

"It's different now." Pinot apprehended his meaning, allowing the wasteland to wash over her, its dull plain like the surface of an alien planet.

Never you. Never again. I'll keep that part.

Pinot grimaced. "Thanks."

It felt like they had traveled for eons, and at the same time, had never moved at all. That this land was an endless loop. The only way to track their progress was the time of day. When it was time to eat. When it was time to sleep. They walked it in their dreams.

Brittni Brinn

Chapter 3
That Promise

As they shivered, half-asleep, arms wrapped around themselves inside their coats, their backs pressing against each other, Ed remembered.

Four years ago, they were with Jax and his tribe of Survival Units, moving up a narrow pathway through the woods, following the candles. Candles in windows, astounding after so long in the wasteland, where nothing grew, where no one lived. Through the night dark, Ed could make out the irregular edges of the walls, the building's resemblance to a hunting lodge. Back before the world disappeared, he'd been to similar wilderness hideouts, where his bosses spent summers drinking champagne, savoring the rustic appearance while experiencing none of its risk.

Jax, baring his wolfish grin, instructed the SUs to stay outside. Jax turned to Pinot, who returned the grin. The two of them were close, their feelings on the same spectrum. May had pointed it out the night the SUs had first appeared: *In my head, there are all these tones. There's one that's similar to yours, Pinot.* And that tone had turned out to be Jax, the leader of a rival gang, with his short mohawk haircut, his cocky arrogance. For a while, they were all afraid of him. His motives were unclear. It was May who'd convinced Ed to control Jax, to keep him from hurting Pinot.

Ed remembered what it was like to close his eyes and spin through Jax's neural pathways. How it felt to turn Jax's head as Pinot walked by. One night, when Jax was walking past the truck bed where Pinot slept, Ed had caused his legs to give out. Ed had aligned Jax's breathing with Pinot's, tried to create a sense of empathy between them.

He remembered the satisfaction he felt when Jax didn't fight his suggestions. That's all they ever were. Ed never manipulated Jax's mind, never tried to control his feelings. That was why it hurt so much when Jax started pursuing Pinot on his own, when he started to love her. Ed never wanted it to go that far. But he couldn't stop it from happening. Pinot and Jax. Their lives were tuned to similar tones. Once they waded through the ocean of blood between them, they understood each other.

Ed learned later that May had influenced him. That she'd used her emotional hearing, or whatever it was, to make him do what she wanted. To control Jax. To protect Pinot. Even when Ed was fevered, close to complete exhaustion from constant use of his electrical ability. Even when he was too weak to stand on his own. Really, he should be the one hating May. But Pinot had lost more than he had. She'd lost a soulmate. Ed had only lost himself.

That long-ago night, it was Jax and Pinot who had led the way through the heavy door into the room beyond. A banquet hall. A summer camp common room. A dance floor. It reminded him of all these things. And the round tables, the scattered chairs. Who was left to use them anymore?

Arissa welcomed him. She read the confession he scribbled out, and as soon as she looked up from the receipt paper, he knew what he had to do. He pulled Jax aside. Maybe he should have waited to tell him, maybe he should have chosen a table closer to the group. Before he could second guess himself, he wrote it all down, finishing with that promise:

I'm not going to do this. Not to you, not to anyone, ever again. I promise you.

He remembered Jax's face, lit from below, the orange

candlelight running over his cheeks, leaving his eyes in shadow. How his teeth gripped together, the way his chin shivered, how his hair shook over his forehead. How Jax had stared at Pinot, sitting on the floor next to Arissa. And then back to Ed as rage overtook him. Ed remembered the heaviness of the blow to his temple, the burning as he sunk into an inky pool, fire licking at the surface.

Pinot was just learning what her healing ability could do but that night she responded like a doctor, putting aside her own feelings to help him. Pinot later told him with a self-deprecating laugh that she had repeated "Don't let him die" to herself as a kind of mantra the whole time she treated his wound to keep her mind off of Jax, who had turned his back on them all, disappearing into the woods with his colony of SUs.

She could have run after him. She could have decided to continue west. She could have let Ed die.

He made that promise to Jax, but Pinot was the reason he kept it. It was why he was here now. Because she chose to stay. He owed her more than he could ever express.

"Did you see that?" Pinot shifted, finding a more comfortable place against his back. "A shooting star. With a green tail, I've never seen one like that before."

He looked up without arching his back. There were so many stars. Smeared thick as glitter on navy construction paper. He took a quick survey of the wasteland—a spill of black, ink over ink.

Brittni Brinn

Chapter 4
Four

A sudden noise startled them awake. Joined at the shoulders, four arms, two-headed, four lungs stinging with the shock of air. Four eyes darted around them, taking in the ring of Grafters. Some with makeshift weapons, some with bandanas and ragged scarves tied around the bottoms of their faces.

"Stand up," a man with glasses ordered.

They broke apart, feeling the pain of separation as they remembered their own bodies, felt the cold close around their exposed legs and backs as they scrambled up.

"The world is a strange place, isn't it?" the Grafter continued. He recognized Pinot, and stepped towards her, taking her arm.

Pinot gritted her teeth, trying to pierce through the man's silver rimmed lenses, discover his intentions.

He nodded at Ed, and another Grafter, the woman with a makeshift spear prodded him forwards.

"Blindfold them."

The two others, one with short blond hair falling over their eyes, another with their brown hair pulled up in a knot, took care of Ed, and then Pinot.

"Walk."

Pinot could hear Ed's unstable breathing, behind her to the left. There wasn't much else they could do but go with the Grafters. There were four of them. Pinot pictured them in the darkness: the two blindfolders, the woman with the spear, the Grafter with glasses. None of them reminded her of the man holding Rhonda's satchel.

The rag over her eyes smelled like vinegar, and she nearly gagged on the smear of sweat she could feel curling in her nostrils. She'd forgotten how grimy the wasteland was, the unwashed clothes, bodies, hair. The smell of festering wounds and rotten teeth. She may have hated Nick's daily hygiene rituals, but those possibilities were beyond her now. A few more days, and she would grow used to the smell, the dirt under her fingernails, the oily skin on her face. A stab of compassion for the Grafters, but she quickly stanched that wound. No need for her to bleed for these people who could be marching her and Ed to their deaths.

Every so often, a pair of hands stopped her at the shoulders, spun her until she was dizzy. A childish strategy, trying to disorient them. A game of blind man's bluff. She guessed they were heading north, but she could be wrong.

A couple of hours passed. Her feet throbbed, the inside of her mouth tingled with thirst. There was a water bottle in her pocket, but she didn't want to fumble for it and expose her knife. They hadn't taken anything from her. The backpack strained against her shoulders, cutting her momentum forwards. None of the Grafters complained. They were silent, only the crunch of their boots on the dirt to remind her of their presence. And the hands, a different set each time, spinning her and letting her stumble. Picking her up. Reorienting her.

A yell from ahead. She heard the Grafter with glasses talking, a bright baritone, and the bass response. They passed by the second voice and she smelled something through the stench of vinegar. Something spicy, sizzling in a pan. Hunger yawned inside her.

She sensed Ed next to her and reached for his hand. A shift in light, a darkening, they were *inside*.

But inside what?

More hands pressed them into sitting shoulder to shoulder.

Their blindfolds were removed.

Pinot wiped at her eyes, imagining the smell coming away like dirt. It remained embedded in her skin, her hair. They were in a tent of some kind, a tarp strung across the doorway. Daylight stripped across the ground, let in through the seams. There was nothing else in the tent except a stack of crates in the corner.

"You okay?" she whispered to Ed. He gripped her hand.

After a few minutes, the Grafter with glasses ducked under the tarp. "Hello again," he said. "Time to see what you've brought us."

There was another Grafter with him, the blindfolder with blonde hair.

"I'm Julius," he sat across from them. "This is Lily." The blonde Grafter didn't sit down. Instead, they placed their palms together. "They have a bit of a gift that I thought would come in handy. I hope you don't mind." Julius took off his glasses, and wiped each lens on his shirt. "Let's start with you."

As Julius reached for Ed's backpack, Pinot held up her hands. At least, she wanted to. Something was keeping her arms from raising.

"Don't try it," Lily said. Their voice was gravel and glass. Pinot tried to open her mouth to reply, but nothing happened.

"Lily can keep you in stasis as long as necessary. However, this would go a lot quicker if you cooperate?" Julius took a moment to look both Pinot and Ed in the eyes before Pinot felt released.

"Do you have any weapons?" Julius asked.

Ed shook his head. Pinot hesitated, then put her left hand in her pocket.

"Slowly," Julius warned. Lily was attentive to her every move.

Pinot held up her other hand as she drew the switchblade and set it on the ground.

"An excellent start." Julius picked up the knife and set it behind him. "Now, take off your jackets."

He went through each pocket, setting some things behind

him, others in a beat-up green crate to his right.

Pinot's face grew hot as he went through her backpack. All of their rations went to his right. He smiled momentarily when he got to the bottom of her bag. "A book many assassins carried with them," he said, placing it in front of Pinot. "Should I be worried?"

Julius didn't wait for an answer. He gave each of them a long look. Pinot and Ed were still wearing their sweaters, their pants, their shoes. This was the threshold, the line she would not cross. Stasis ability be damned. She squeezed Ed's hand and he sent one in return. They were agreed. This would go no further. They'd fight their way out if necessary.

Julius watched this exchange and set Pinot's bag behind him. He nodded to Lily. The blonde Grafter hefted up the crate and left the tent.

"Now," Julius shuffled closer to them, "we have a lot to talk about." He rubbed his hands together. "Lily doesn't like it when I do this, but I think it's important for us to have a little privacy."

Pinot and Ed watched, their shoulders tense, each waiting for a signal from the other.

Julius faced his palms outward, as if bracing against two walls in a narrow alleyway. Pinot started to sweat in the suddenly warm air. She glanced at Ed, arrested by the distinctness of each thread in his sweatshirt, the grubby grey now shining with a sheen of steel. Julius' glasses looked as if they'd been drawn on, the frames surreally sharp.

"What the hell?" Pinot said, and immediately covered her mouth. Even her words sounded highlighted, brighter. She didn't recognize her own voice.

"I've been told that from the outside, it looks as if we're in a giant glass aquarium, filled with smoke." Julius calmly sat back, leaning his weight on his hands. Blocking Pinot's view of her switchblade, gleaming on the dirt. "No one can hear us."

Ed stretched a hand out beside him; there was no difference, no resistance.

A thrill of fear ran up Pinot's neck, but she suppressed it.

Julius hadn't moved any closer to them. In fact, he'd relaxed slightly, the intimidating throw of his shoulders and harshness of his jaw giving way to a readiness.

"What do you want?"

Julius quirked an eyebrow. "Nothing. You saw Reah out there, her arm's fine. Infection completely gone. So, I figure I owe you one."

Pinot felt Ed's eyes on her. "A Grafter I helped out a while back," she explained. "But the other one, the one who took my friend's bag?"

"He moved on."

Pinot closed her eyes against the amplified force of Julius' voice. When she opened them, his face was grim, a blood vessel standing out on his forehead.

"Anyway, that's not important," Julius said, returning to his relaxed posture, "Where you headed?"

Brittni Brinn

Chapter 5
Formulaic

Ed repocketed a wad of scrap paper and his favorite blue bic pen. The pen was running out of ink. Back before the Event, he'd drop by Staples on his way home, pick up a pack of 20. They'd exist in a jumble on his desk, and he'd toss them into a garbage bin on the other side of his office when they couldn't keep up with his ideas. Now, he hoarded them. Every stub of pencil. Every cracked pen. Without them, he was wordless.

Julius had gone out to find them food. Pinot was fidgeting with her switchblade, elbows on knees, dark hair falling over her eyes. Julius must be serious if he was letting her keep the weapon, along with everything from the pile behind him. About them getting to Summerland in one piece, that was. Otherwise, the man was hard to read.

Ed thought of how he could write this into a video game. It was formulaic if he looked at it the right way: the protagonist leaves the safety of their home, goes out into the dangerous unknown. Is captured and questioned. What next? A daring escape? A bargain is made? The leader of the rebels is some kind of long lost brother, so of course, he can't really hurt them? Ed stopped himself. No point in going on. There wouldn't be any more video games, he remembered. Not for a long time.

Lily pushed the tarp aside, carrying two camping bowls and a full water bottle. "Here you are," they said, their voice less gravel, more steady asphalt. They handed Pinot and Ed a bowl and set the water bottle down between them. "It's a curry, don't ask me where Asin found the ingredients. You can sleep here tonight."

"Who's Asin?" Pinot asked, turning the closed blade over in her hands.

"You'll meet him." Lily smiled at Ed, cutting through the ruggedness of their smooth face. "Enjoy the food." They left the way they came.

Pinot spit into the water bottle, into each of the bowls. They scooped the curry in their fingers. It wasn't enough, but they filled their stomachs with water to make themselves forget.

The seams of the tent went dark. Ed and Pinot settled into their routine. Back to back. Pinot facing the tarp, knife in her hand. Ed facing the back of the tent, in case of infiltration. They half-slept, half-lived in a waking dream.

Chapter 6
New

The next day, Lily gave them a tour of the settlement. The tent where they'd spent the night was one of a dozen pitched in a semi-circle around a well.

"You have a well!" Pinot exclaimed, as Ed leaned over the crude fence built around it, looking for the bottom. "Who built this?"

Lily introduced them to Asin, the closest thing the camp had to a leader. He was stocky, midway into his 40s, with a long black braid and a shaved face. "Asin built our well," Lily said, nodding solemnly to Asin, a sign of respect for his accomplishment.

Asin returned the nod and went back to the rip in a sleeve he was mending. The old winter coat was torn in several places, not padded, but made of thick brown cloth tightly woven and lined with what looked like sheep wool.

"We're all starting to get ready." Lily's breath hung in the air around their face. Their blonde hair was cut short, and they showed a slight 5 o'clock shadow. Their clothes were plain and utilitarian, a scarf with tasseled ends wrapped snugly under their chin.

"Lily," Pinot said, "are you all Grafters?"

"We call ourselves Foragers here," they replied, glancing at Pinot out of the corners of their brilliant blue eyes. "There used to be more."

"There were families here, weren't there?" A child's bicycle stuck out from a scrap pile they passed.

"This isn't a place for children."

"Too dangerous."

Lily nodded. "Families went to Summerland. It's why we have such a good relationship with the settlement."

Pinot scanned the camp. "How many of you were together, when it happened?"

"The Event, that was a long time ago." Lily's eyes narrowed, as if in warning.

"Five years isn't that long."

"Another lifetime. Where so much was possible."

"Did you and Julius—"

"That's enough." Lily stalked ahead, leading them between a couple of tents to a workshop area. Old doors acted as tables, spanning stacks of crates, logs, stools. A few Foragers patched a tarp. Another tinkered with a spoked wheel. None of them looked up from their work and Lily didn't stop to introduce Pinot and Ed. A Forager standing next to one of the worktables glared at them. Her grey blonde hair was secured in a bun, pulling her ivory skin tight at the temples. "How dare you!" The Forager pointed a sharp fingernail at Lily. "How dare you bring these outsiders into our home!"

The people around her lowered their tools, some with a smirk, some sharing worried glances.

"No need for the bravado, Phyllis." Lily faced the Forager, hands clasped loosely in front of them.

Phyllis blinked. "I assure you that I'm only saying what everyone here is thinking. This kind of foolish risk is putting our whole community in danger. The outsiders can't be trusted, can't you see that?"

"They're here for a reason."

"Is that so." Phyllis placed her hands on her hips. "Why don't you tell us what it is?"

"At the next meeting—"

"Who made you the decision makers?"

The Foragers around her shifted, some throwing their shoulders back. Some picked up their tools and left. Only a handful moved closer to Lily, facing Phyllis alongside them.

"Seems strange to me that you get to keep information from us. Isn't this a group where everyone is equal?"

"If you have a problem with me, Phyllis, take it up with Asin."

"Oh, I will. This looks bad on you, and on Julius too, might I add. And you two—" she jabbed her fingernail at Pinot and Ed— "you'd have been better off if you'd never seen this place."

"Come on," Lily spoke quietly, and turned away from Phyllis and the other Foragers.

We could just leave, Ed wrote as he and Pinot hurried to catch up.

"Not yet. I want to know more about this place. About these people."

Why?

Pinot grinned as she noticed a woman holding a spear. "Because they're new."

Chapter 7
Reah

Reah rested her spear in the crook of her arm, the sharp point hovering overhead, the butt of it grounding her as she waited to relieve one of the camp's sentries. She stretched her other arm in front of her. The shape of it was lost in the bulky sleeve of her plaid jacket; underneath were scars, but no more infection. Barbed wire, she'd told Julius after it happened, what she'd kept telling him until she told him the truth.

Their group had been foraging around an abandoned farmhouse about a week away from camp. While Reah and Thomas pried boards from the porch, Julius had gone to check out a shed on the other side of the overgrown yard. As soon as they were alone, Thomas had tried, he'd lured her into the kitchen, pinning her against the fridge. She'd smashed a plate across his jaw, but he'd caught up to her and thrown her off the porch. She'd landed arm first on a pile of discarded boards, felt the teeth and the sharp intake of nails, splinters, fire. But she couldn't wait there, she'd picked herself up, ripped the pain from her bare upper arm. Into the overgrowth, stumbling, the blood running warm. She'd huddled in the overblown wheat and weeds that had worked their way into the field.

She'd heard Julius and Thomas talking close by. She'd pushed herself up, followed Julius's warm voice. And she'd stayed quiet, hadn't told Julius, because Thomas was dangerous, and there were only the three of them and they had supplies to bring back to camp. And with her down one arm...

At first Julius had believed her story about running into barbed wire while searching the underbrush for equipment. But as the days went by, he'd noticed the berth she gave Thomas, and she'd wanted him to notice. It would make telling him easier.

The day they met the healer, Reah had been ready to run off, take her wound and keep everyone else the way they were. But the healer had seen through her, gave Thomas, who stood there clutching a messenger bag, a look like she had so often wanted to give him. One that carried with it a knowing, an accusation, a warning. And Julius had noticed it too.

The next day, when Julius was rewrapping her arm, he'd said, "The healer didn't seem to like Thomas much."

She could've laughed it off. But Julius was asking her for more, the way he'd said it. So she'd told him.

And that night, Julius had taken her spear while she slept and had driven it through Thomas's skull.

Reah only had bursts of memory from the days that followed. Trying to remember the rest was like using an unfocused telescope to find craters on the moon. But she could clearly recall one conversation— when she woke up to find Julius burying Thomas's body.

"You shouldn't have done that!" she'd nearly screamed at him.

"Reah—"

"You'll get in trouble!"

"I won't—"

"We're supposed to take problems to the group. It's one of the rules!"

"Reah, listen. He hurt you. I wasn't going to let him hurt you again."

"What if Asin sends you away? What if I never see you again?"

"It's worth it to make sure you're safe." Julius had straightened then, his hands caked in the chalk-like dirt of the wasteland.

"Don't tell."

"What?"

"Say Thomas went away. Don't tell."

"Are you sure?"

Reah was sure. She still was.

The surface of her arm was marked with scars, which made Reah think of the healer. When they'd met in the wasteland, the woman had introduced herself as a doctor, but Reah knew well enough that she was too young, that water and some homemade pills wouldn't be enough to flush out the infection spreading from the crusted red-black gashes on her arm. Still, Julius had done what the healer had said, to the letter. After a week, they'd unwrapped the gauze, gasping because the wounds had closed, leaving only glossy scars.

There were enough strange things they could accept now, that they could accept this. Julius' ability to create "safe rooms", for example. Or Lily's "stasis." They were adept at it now, the powers that had at first been difficult to control. Reah remembered Lily and Julius walking hand in hand that first year, and Julius suddenly freezing in place. How Lily's face would flush with embarrassment, how Julius would laugh and kiss Lily once they'd released him.

The healer was coming towards Reah now. Her friend with electrified hair next to her, Lily looming over the two of them like a pillar of gold smoke. Being shown around, like Julius had asked. Reah was relieved. Asin could have thrown them out, but here they were, getting the grand tour.

"Hello," the healer said as the group reached her, "glad to hear the arm healed up." Her eyes were black holes, only a hint of space's lighter dark in her irises. A discolored patch of skin around one eye ran up into her hairline, drawing the color from it as well. A shock of white sweeping her forehead, the milky way. An entire galaxy in the strands of her hair.

"Reah?" Lily's hand lowered onto her shoulder, their voice concerned.

"Yeah, thanks, I mean thank you. I'm really…. You and your friends, we didn't hurt you did we? We didn't hurt anybody!"

"I understand."

"Yeah, okay, thanks. I mean, I'm glad too."

The healer nodded, her hands deep in her pockets. "This is Ed, I don't think you've met yet."

"What about the other two? The ones we… sorry, sorry."

"They're fine. Not with us though."

"No, just the two of you."

"Yeah." The healer smiled at her, but not really with her mouth. More with the space around her eyes, a relaxing of her shoulders.

Reah crossed her arms and tried to smile back.

"Can I ask you something?" The healer wanted to see her arm.

"Yeah, yeah sure." Reah drew her arm out from her plaid coat, rolled up the short t-shirt sleeve underneath.

The healer stepped closer to her, slowly pressed on the scars. "Why are these still here?" the healer muttered under her breath, but then stepped back and nodded. "Shouldn't give you any more problems."

Reah threaded her arm back into her coat. She watched the three of them as they moved away. She held the healed arm in front of her inside of the plaid sleeve. "Why are these still here?" she repeated and wrapped both arms around herself against the cold.

Chapter 8
Time to Talk

It was time to talk with the newcomers. Asin decided this while standing next to the well, sipping from an ice-edged cup as he watched dawn streak across the wasteland. No one else was up, just a couple of camp members on watch who stretched and paced, their breath going up like fine smoke in the cold. Asin felt the shiver in his chest and hung the cup on a hook curling from a fractured fencepost. Curling, like a question mark boring itself into the exclamation of the wood, the thick splinters repeating a thousand-fold. Asin's aunt would've looked into it, maybe, this passing observation, searching deep into its everyday symbolism for a kernel of meaning.

But not Asin. Even if he did think this wasteland was on another plane, he trusted his senses for what they were meant for, not what he could make up about them. They showed him the material, whereas the immaterial was unseen inside each of them. It had manifested into what were commonly called abilities, but Asin disliked the term. As if the people without them, like himself, were less without them, were without ability.

Instead, he called them manifests. They were the metaphysical energy inside of people that the Event had given form to. Allowed it to be channeled into the material world, so the person could manifest their energy and use it. Not an ability. A skill, a gift even. But even gift was tricky: who had given the gift? Were they earned? At least skills could be learned; the label acknowledged the fact that the manifests needed practice in order to be understood and strengthened. That overusing them could actually harm the manifest, like overworking a muscle. Even though Julius disagreed with him, Asin could find no better way of thinking about the strange things people could now initiate.

Asin waited a few more hours before visiting the newcomers. He took over a watch, worked on a new stretching rack he was developing for drying animal hides. When he couldn't wait any longer, he walked through the camp and sat outside their tent. He whittled at a stick he had with him, shaping it into a fine whistle with narrow finger stops and an angled mouthpiece. It was nearly an hour later that he heard Pinot's voice, and movement in the tent.

"'Morning," he called from where he was sitting, "have a good sleep?"

"Yes," Pinot responded, "is that Asin out there?"

"I wondered if you'd like to have breakfast together."

Pinot's voice lowered and conferred with Ed. Then she drew the tarp in the doorway aside and nodded to him, still bleary-eyed, stretching out her back. Julius had told him that Pinot slept sitting up, watching for intruders. A little paranoid, given how kindly they'd welcomed them. Asin smiled, taking note of how Pinot held the way open for Ed. They had their belongings with them. Didn't trust the camp, he noted. If nothing else, the newcomers were tenacious.

***

Ed followed Pinot and Asin through the camp. They stopped by the food station. Reah was taking a shift, mixing a package of chicken noodle soup with a rotund can of tomatoes, adding equal parts boiled water to stretch it out enough for everyone. Breakfast used to mean dried cereal and instant coffee, but Ed didn't mind the change. He noticed that even though Pinot was basically sleepwalking, she welcomed the small bowl of soup she was handed.

They all walked slow and careful so as not to spill their food. Asin led them into his tent. Ed noted that it was barely more furnished than their own. The only difference was a rolled up sleeping bag set on a crate and a weathered wooden desk stashed in the corner. The three of them sat on the floor and drank their soup.

"When will your Foraging team be heading out?" Pinot asked for Ed, who had handed her the question.

"Once the other party returns. We'll get everyone settled for winter before my team takes their turn."

Ed nodded seriously. *Makes sense.*

"Seems like a good system you got going here. Though I am curious how you came to be the leader."

"Who says I'm the leader?"

"Lily, for one. And Phyllis seems to care about your opinion."

Asin took a thoughtful sip of soup. "Anyone could be the leader here. That's the beauty of the shift system. It's all shared evenly. We work out our problems as they come up, together."

"Fucking paradise," Pinot grinned, setting her empty bowl aside.

"I'm not particularly happy Julius brought you here, as you can probably tell. This is supposed to be a closed camp, with very few exceptions."

"He must've thought we'd be useful."

"You, specifically."

"Why's that?"

Asin sighed. "Julius and Reah told me about her injury, about you treating her. They say you're not a doctor, you're a healer."

"So?"

"I prefer to call them manifests: your manifest is healing; Julius's manifest creates silent rooms, Lily's can freeze physical actions."

"Maybe." Pinot looked to Ed who nodded. They'd decided to ask Asin a question that could be dangerous. "Are the abilities here...the manifests, are they fading? Getting weaker? I've treated people in the past who said that their abilities have been getting less effective."

Asin studied Pinot's face. "Nothing like that here. I can't speak for myself, but as far as I know Julius and Lily's manifests are the same as they were three years ago."

"Three years ago. Is that when they started?"

"That's when we met and started this camp."

"I see." But Pinot didn't, and raised her dark eyebrows at Ed.

Ed shrugged slightly in response. It didn't make sense. Why should their abilities be breaking down but not others?

"Now, if you're going to be staying a while, I'd like to go over our camp rules." Asin opened a tattered notebook and set it in front of them.

1. *Act in the best interest of the camp.*

2. *Do no harm to your fellow camp mates.*

3. *All supplies are to be split equally as possible and are to be used in the way that benefits the whole camp the most. In the case of food, all food will be given to the food tent to be distributed to everyone.*

4. *Infractions will be punished by the group.*

5. *The only infractions punishable by death: the murder of a camp mate; the rape of a camp mate.*

"Remember those," Asin said as he closed the notebook and held out a hand for their empty dishes, "and we'll all get along fine."

Chapter 9
Subterranean

That afternoon, Julius led Pinot and Ed out from the core of the camp. Around the cluster of tents was a half-ring of gaping holes in the ground, each framed with thick wooden beams like the entrances to coal mines. A few metres down one of the descending paths into the earth, they came up against a ridge, a giant's step into what looked like a storage closet. Stacked green crates covered one of the walls, bits of fabric and gleams of glass showing through the plastic, and a musty smell, like dried vegetables, filled the foyer. A green sheet hung ahead of them, and they followed Julius around it into the room beyond. It was small but dug deep enough that they could stand almost fully upright. A cooking fire warmed the center of the room, smoke curling up and out through a vent in the ceiling. More beams stabilized the walls on either side of the dugout.

"Subterranean shelter," Julius stopped near one of the dirt walls, placing a hand on the packed surface. "The earth insulates it. Cold air from the tunnel gets caught against that big step you saw on the way in. Asin learned how to make them when he was living up north, before the Event."

"This is really something else," Pinot's voice was faded, grubby with lack of sleep. After a couple quiet nights and the security of having something overhead, Ed had started to curl on his side, hip and shoulder digging into the ground, his arm cushioning his head going numb. He figured the sore muscles the next day were worth the relief of waking up refreshed. But Pinot still spent her nights propped up against the pile of crates with her coat tucked around her. As a result, Pinot went through her days with her eyes half-closed and she sometimes took an extra couple of seconds to respond to his notes or when someone asked her a question. Ed considered ways to convince her that he could keep watch, so she could slip into a proper REM cycle. She was the doctor here, she should know better.

"We spent a couple months underground last year. The best part is that from far away, they don't stand out. The smoke could tip passing travellers off, but most don't make it that close to the camp."

"What do you do for food?"

"Keep as much preserved food as possible during the year. We hunt. Traders from Summerland come through once the worst of the winter is over. We keep a stock of items we know they need, and they bring us food. It's a useful agreement. They don't have to come far, and we don't starve."

Ed set himself down next to the fire, looking up through the vent. What would a whole winter be like, huddled in here? he wondered. It was a lot warmer than up on the surface. Smelled homey, like bread and peat and wool blankets. Wouldn't be so bad.

Pinot leaned on one of the pillars. "Why are you showing us this?"

"I guess," Julius said after a moment, "that I'm trying to convince you to stay."

Stay here? Ed quirked an eyebrow in Pinot's direction.

Pinot sat down next to Ed, her shoulders slumping with relief at not having to stand any longer. She fought off a bout of exhaustion as Ed watched, her eyelids sliding shut, flashing open again.

"You want us to stay?"

Julius nodded, but only at Pinot. Ed knew the reason. "You took care of Reah's arm. You're a healer—"

"I'm not—"

"You have *experience*." Julius knelt across the campfire from them, his hands raised as if for warmth. What he was really saying was *Wait. Don't make up your mind just yet.* "If you stayed, we could spend the winter learning from it. You could show us how to identify certain illnesses. How to staunch a wound, how to tie up a broken bone. When you saw Reah's injuries, you immediately knew they were infected. Some of us don't know how to do that. And the rest of us don't really know enough." He laughed, the baritone ring dampened by the earthen walls. "It's amazing any of us are still alive at all."

"It's hard for life to kill us." Pinot said after a moment, her voice low. "But once it's happened to someone you know, it seems impossibly easy." She pulled her knees up to her chin, pocketed her hands.

"Yes." Julius' comment was quiet, and the two of them stared into the fire as Ed looked up and out through the vent above them. A sliver of washed-out blue.

Brittni Brinn

Chapter 10
Pinot's Dream

Pinot couldn't remember the last time she had dreamed. It was one of the reasons she welcomed the nights of half sleep, her tailbone aching, the chill wrapping its way through her coat. She spent her nights in this half-state, paralyzed with the fear that the pile of crates she rested against would shift off-balance and rain down, burying her alive. In the daylight, her fear evaporated with one look at the nearly weightless plastic, each jigsawed to the bottom, top, and sides of the crates around it. But she shrunk in the dark, and the crates continued up forever, and she could hear Ed's uneven breathing across the room. The cold, the crates, Ed's breathing—cycles that lasted eternities. Even this was preferable to what was waiting for her in her dreams.

Last night, she'd slipped from the crates, must've curled on her side. The deepest sleep in weeks.

She dreamed she was on the edge of a shale cliff, bare rock and scree. One foot bracing her, compressing as she leaned forward trying to see over the lip into the deep, deep down. There was a smell in the air, a stinging, pungent smell—sharp salt and seaweed, rotting flesh.

A primal fear gripped her as the throw of her gaze cleared the edge and tumbled down into a tumult of white crests on black water. Waves broke over rocks, hurling themselves against the cliff wall. Her tears plummeted, hit the far off sea with crackles like fireworks and sparks of blue light. "Did you make it?" she asked.

Suddenly, her foot slipped, she was falling, wind ripping her clothes and her skin to shreds. A sharp intake as she felt the second before impact. A wall of water pushed her down, everything bubbling chaos.

The black water settled. She floated upwards, her hair floating around her like tendrils of seaweed. The underside of the surface approached, and she saw a reflection of herself, her body whole and shining black, her face covered in scars, her hair flaring white like a comet aura.

She breached the ocean surface, felt the water clear from her skin. The sea was calm. Her first view of the sky was dim purple, the far-off cliff wowing in and out of the top of her vision. Warm seawater buoyed her body. For a time, she floated, peaceful.

But then she started to think about how far away land was, how she would have to climb the shale cliff to return home. It was too far.

So I'll stay, she thought. I'll heal the ocean.

Without warning, the water around her surged, lifted her into the air, pushed her to her feet. The cliff top approached, and the pillar of water arced towards it, leaving her where she'd started. She scrambled to the edge, watching the stream lose consistency as it fell back into the sea as a torrent of rain.

Her heart pounded in her head. Another pillar surged from the surface, hundreds of feet. She only had a moment to recognize that there was a figure riding this one as well: a head of black hair, a narrow body, a young man. He stood on the pillar of water, parallel to her. His torso was covered in silver and blue scales. Anemones and coral curled across his bare chest and arms, his legs glowed a dim bioluminescent.

Only his face was flesh. His hair was the same as she remembered, a short mohawk, the front of it tumbling down over his narrowed eyes, his high cheekbones, his sharpened eyeteeth. She stretched a hand out for him, but there was too much distance. He saw her intention and shook his head, his mouth twisting in disgust.

"You're just like the rest of them," he said. He jumped impossibly high, flipping his body, diving headfirst into the stream of water.

"I'm not!" she yelled after him, shivering. The pillar of water sunk away from her as he swam down it into the deep, deep dark. "I'm not! I'm not!"

Brittni Brinn

Chapter 11
Loners

"I'm not!" Pinot yelled, and Ed rolled to his feet, following her voice through the spots that swam over his vision. He knew the usual outcome of this dream: she would wake up with damp eyes, swallowing a sob into her chest.

Ed knelt facing her curled body, shook her shoulder. Wake up, he thought at her, it's okay Pinot, wake up.

Seeming to sense him, she took a deep breath. She shifted, falling into a different sleep, dreamless.

Ed sat back, waiting in case the nightmare returned. Pinot slept, her face buried in the angle of her arm, her knees pulled close to her chest. She was fully dressed, all blacks and navys and greys, nothing that would stand out in the wasteland, her hair dark brown except for the section of white that never grew in the same. She looked vulnerable like this, not the tough punk, not the desperate doctor who'd stabbed a man in the head and pulled out his entrails. Ed swallowed a sadness of his own, thinking of how lonely she was. How they both were.

But that's why we're here, he thought as he pushed himself up and brushed his hands on the front of his canvas jacket, we're not the kind of people who fit in.

He squinted a little against the sunlight and cold as he exited the tent. Not many people were out. Most were getting ready to go underground. He stopped at the well, took the cup hanging on the fence post and filled it. Flecks of ice floated through his mouth, scathed his throat on the way down.

Ed realized his forehead was furrowed and released the tension between his eyebrows, took a breath. Would staying really be the best option? Winter would soon be in full force, and they wouldn't get far once the flurries started. Snow itself wasn't the problem. It tended to localize around the forest and the small settlements scattered across the sterile plain. On the wasteland, it was more the wind you had to watch for. Out there, it was frostbite and snow blindness and wearing down. Nothing to burn, nothing to eat.

At least they'd have shelter in the Forager camp. He felt the tension in his forehead return. Phyllis hadn't been alone in her feelings about outsiders. He and Pinot still felt the glares on their backs when they made the short trip from their tent to get food. They could press on to Summerland, Pinot knew a couple of people there from past medical runs. They'd treat her well.

What's so interesting about this place, anyway? Ed thought, immediately realizing pretty much everything. The well they dug themselves, the underground houses. He'd never seen anything like this. A camp built up from nothing. Most communities he'd heard about from Pinot had started in an abandoned building, with some infrastructure already in place. This, this was unheard of. These Foragers were of a different stuff.

Ed stretched, then rested his forearms on the fence around the well. He buried his face deeper into his scarf, an old gift from Victoria. When she'd given it to him two winters ago, the bright whites and blues looked unworn. Maybe she'd made it. He couldn't remember. An image of her teasing smile as she nailed a new set of boards along the outside of the shed crossed his mind. He thought back on her with a sad affection, wondering what could've been different, knowing the outcome would have remained unchanged.

Lily came out from the tent they shared with Julius, walked down to the well. Ed handed them the communal cup, and they accepted it without a word. Lily's face was thin and long with a strong chin and blue eyes. Their blonde bangs were tucked under a toque. They were wearing the same coat as before, black wool down to their knees, thick black buttons. A muted pashmina shawl was wrapped loosely around their shoulders.

"Do you smoke?" they asked him. Ed shook his head, making a kind of hopeless motion with his hands. Even if he did, cigarettes were almost impossible to come by.

Lily removed a couple of pencil-thin paper tubes from a case in their pocket, offered him one. "I make my own," Lily explained, flicking a cheap plastic lighter and holding the tiny flame to the end of each cigarette. "Try it."

Ed did. It definitely wasn't tobacco; the herbal aftertaste was pleasant, soothing. The smoke rushing out from the corners of his mouth brought with it the memory of cigars he'd smoked years ago. Never more than one a night, and only at parties. Standing in a circle on some balmy outdoor porch. On the floor with the windows open. A deep whisper. Conspiratorial laughter. Smoke mingling as it dissipated into memory.

He took another draw, nodded appreciatively. He smiled over at Lily, a little embarrassed. In the old days, he'd tell anecdotes to repay the provider of the cigars.

"Glad you like it. Julius doesn't approve, you see. He's a bit of a health nut." Lily's thin eyebrows arched up past the brim of their toque.

Ed and Lily laughed at the ridiculous idea of trying to be healthy in times like these. Ed could tell Lily about all of the fad dieters and organic foodies he used to know, the strange health crazes his coworkers would follow to the letter, even if it meant drinking prune juice instead of coffee in the mornings. Instead, they both leaned against the fence and finished their cigarettes.

Ed wrote *Thank you* on a scrap of paper and handed it to Lily. They read it, said "No problem," and headed back to their tent. Ed watched them, the broad shoulders and deliberate steps, thinking that if there was one person he had to trust in this camp, it would be Lily.

Chapter 12
On Watch

Over the next couple of days, Ed and Pinot managed to piece together how the Forager camp functioned. The Foragers who volunteered to scavenge were split into three shifts. Julius' shift was the one that brought Pinot and Ed in from the wasteland. Asin led another—his group was set to leave as soon as the third one returned. This was the camp's routine. A shift headed out in a new direction, only as far as necessary. It could be a patch of land, half of a community center, a wanderer in the waste. They would scavenge, take what they needed, as much as they could, and return.

A shift could be away for days. Sometimes, it took weeks. Sometimes they returned with food, sometimes with supplies, and they marked where they'd been on the communal map Asin kept in his tent or left with Julius when he was out foraging. Ed had seen the map a couple of times: it was sketched out on the first page of a beat-up notebook, the cardboard cover half torn from the binding, the pages close to falling out from people flipping back and forth between entries.

The Foragers went back to places they'd been, if the notes said there were still potential supplies. The closest marks had been cleaned out. When that happened, Asin drew a circle around the mark and closed the entry by writing "EMPTY" under the related notes.

The map kept track of trading routes too, in case the camp got desperate. The trading route to Summerland wasn't included. It was their line to survival in the winter, and the rest of the year, they left it alone. A couple of times, they'd even had to protect it. Asin considered it a good use of a shift, so occasionally he sent a group along with the trade caravan to take care of any nuisances.

The camp had one gun, carried by one of the Foragers on watch. Always two sentries, always. Every time of the day and night.

Tonight, it was Ed and Pinot's turn.

Pinot monitored the perimeter, pacing the packed earth to keep warm. She thought that no matter how far you go, it's easy to get stuck someplace. Places like eddies in the stream, and you're like a fish, catching your breath behind a rock. The rapids are brutal and you think just one more minute, but then you wait too long and get trapped in a pool no bigger than you are until the waters run easier. She dug her hiking boots into each step to remind herself that she was not trapped, that she could leave whenever suited her. She'd swam through rougher waters than the wasteland, after all.

Further up the edge of the settlement, Ed sat on one of the many crates that permeated the camp. He was hungry. At the start of their watch, each of them received a bowl of warmed peas, the last of the supplies commandeered from Pinot's backpack. But that food went quickly, and he cast about in his mind for something to distract him from the empty hole in his stomach. He remembered the smell of curry as they walked into camp that first day, how it made his mouth water. He thought of Pavlov's dog, which led to an image of men in old films panting after skirts. The face of a woman quickly cancelled it, her blue-green eyes as clear as the day he last saw her, before the Event carried her away. *Kay.* He could almost grasp the pressure of her body against his, the taste of her mouth. But he was too hungry, he couldn't sustain anything. He let her fade into memory, into a time that would never be again.

Meanwhile, Pinot held the gun, the barrel ice cold to the touch through the palms of her gloves. Asin only barely trusted them with a sentry shift. "If you see anything, you come to me, I'll take care of it." She hadn't seen anything so far. It was complete dark, the camp invisible, no light pollution. She missed the glowing cityscapes of her teenage years, the grungy silhouettes of warehouses, the streetlights burning orange against the night.

Ed was still hungry. Bright spots traversed his vision and he blinked them away. They returned and remained. Suddenly, he realized that they weren't caused by hunger, they weren't in his eyes. The bright spots were *out there*. And they were moving.

He jumped up, scrambling for the crate under him. He banged it against the ground, keeping his eyes on the lights coming slowly towards them.

Pinot ran up beside him, her breath ragged. "What is it— Ed, what the fuck is that?" She gripped the gun and they squinted into the black, uncertain if what they saw was real. Ed was thrown off balance as Pinot abruptly pushed the gun into his arms and took off to intercept the lights.

Pinot recognized these lights, the distance between each one, two galaxies made up of a hundred stars. She felt the strain in her chest as she pushed herself towards them.

Ed ran after her, holding the gun away from him, wondering if the safety was on. He came to a stop behind Pinot, his breath rasping as the two Survival Units approached.

"Over here!" Pinot yelled to them, waving her arms. It was possible that the people inside the SUs were asleep, but she figured that the presence of a human should be enough to sound an alarm inside.

The SUs slowed to a halt a few metres ahead, the plastic-domed sensors set along their exteriors glowing white. Their shells made a double-arced hulk against the dark.

She wondered if the people inside the SUs had the voice scrambler on, a precaution against outsiders. "I've travelled with others like you before," she called, holding her hands out with her palms towards them. Showing she meant no harm. "Are you looking for them? Did Jax send you?"

"Jax?" The response rang hollow through the communicator of the first SU. "You know him?"

"We've only just met him ourselves," the other SU added. "A bit brisk, wasn't he, Jeff?"

"Used to know," Pinot said in answer to Jeff's question. "How did you get a hold of these?"

"Finders keepers," came the second voice, citing the practical rule of the wasteland.

Pinot's mouth formed into an exhilarated grin. "Where are you going?"

"Not sure," the lighter voice continued, "wherever that Jax fellow is leading us."

"Leading you? How?"

"He sent coordinates."

"Autopilot?"

"Yeah, it's wonderful. No work for us at all."

"What are the coordinates?"

"Sorry. Classified."

"Like hell!"

"Sorry."

For a moment, Pinot said nothing, the flare of anger burnt out of her. "How far west did he get?"

"Sorry."

"Let us come with you."

A brief pause.

"Should we ask Jax if you can come along?" Jeff's tone was sobering.

Pinot's shoulders slumped, and her hands went to her pockets. "No... no I guess not."

"Nice to meet you!" the lighter voice said, and the SUs hummed back into motion, passing Pinot and Ed by as they continued their journey.

Ed thought of a hundred things to say to Pinot's defeated shoulders. It's okay. He's not worth it. It's not your fault. But he knew none of them would help. So he waited, keeping an eye on the shrinking lights until they were swallowed by darkness.

Brittni Brinn

Chapter 13
Historiated Initials

Asin's foraging group cast long shadows as they struck east. It was the golden hour, just after dawn, sunlight tumbling across the wasteland like air-thin honey. Every clod of dirt was illuminated. Each tent edged in golden ink. Cold, this filigree, each human figure a historiated initial against the horizon. Each started its own story—to be continued.

Pinot and Ed leaned on the well fence, wearing their coats, their backpacks. Nothing out of the ordinary, since they never left the tent without their belongings. Pinot glanced to Ed, the ends of his red hair reflecting the light, the depths of his hollow cheeks flooded with it. She felt grungy in comparison.

Hiking her pack higher up her shoulders, she pulled her hood low over her face. The two of them weaved around the back of the tents, many of them empty now, the occupants underground. The workshop area had been dismantled, wood chips and discarded tufts of blue tarp littering the ground. Lily sat nearby on a crate, smoking.

As Pinot and Ed stepped through the remnants, Ed paused. He waited for his body to go rigid, immoveable, caught by Lily's stasis ability. When nothing changed he looked over at Lily. They matched his eyes, then shrugged. "It's your decision," they said, and cleared their throat. "Good luck out there."

Pinot and Ed broke off from the camp, the wind's cold

fingers working through their clothes, into their bones. They followed the SUs' trail for an hour before it too went cold.

Ed knew it was pointless. The SUs were self-sustaining machines, meant to withstand extreme temperatures and lack of shelter. They didn't need fuel. They didn't need to rest. He and Pinot were fragile in comparison, already hungry and tired. He hoped that Pinot would come to her senses and take them through Summerland at least. That hope was also pointless. Pinot had found a way back to Jax. And he was bound to follow.

Am I though? he thought, already wanting the floor of the tent, a mouthful of peas. Lily's blue gaze flashed through his mind. He could winter with the camp of Foragers, make his way back to Arissa's come spring. Finish making *Trace of Shadows* and sleep late every morning.

Tempting, isn't it? he laughed internally. Too many things he could do or could've done. But what *was* he doing? What was he doing with his life?

So he wrote a note, waved Pinot back once she realized he'd stopped. *Take a break?*

They sat with their backs to the wind. Pinot took out a granola bar stashed away in her coat for such an event, and they each ate a bite. The oats were dry and there was barely any flavor left in the years-overdue bar. Pinot squinted at the compass, looking back over her shoulder. Ed took out the rough map he'd drawn from memory after seeing the original in Asin's tent.

"Looks like a storehouse of some kind up ahead." Pinot's voice was raspy, having to cut through the wind. "We can spend the night."

Ed nodded, relieved that Pinot didn't want to push through in the dark. The cold was unbearable as it was, and who knew what kind of Grafters were prowling the area.

They pressed on through the wind, taking breaks, eating their way through the whole granola bar. Pinot had one water bottle in her backpack, found near the well and secreted into her baggy hoodie. They'd gotten through half of it, but the rest of the water was frozen.

The mark on the map turned out to be a stand-alone garage, and there was no one inside, to their relief. A small quartered glass window with a broken pane sat high in the back wall. There were signs of an old campfire in the corner, some murky jars on a shelf, and rusted cans scattering the concrete floor. Nothing else.

They started a small fire using matches Pinot had tucked away in an inner pocket and some siding torn off the outside of the garage. Just enough to warm their corner of the room. They thawed the water near the fire, each taking a mouthful.

"Not too bad for the first night," Pinot said, sitting shoulder to shoulder with Ed, their soles facing the fire pit.

He clenched his hand to get the blood flowing, and wrote a quick note.

"Hmm," Pinot read, "I don't know where they're going. But you said you watched them head due west. So that's where we go."

The fire and the warmth of Pinot's shoulder drew the shivering out of him and as his body relaxed, he heard Pinot's voice as if from a distance.

"...I'll wake you in a couple hours."

The bare inside of the garage door and the skeletal steel tracks looming above faded, along with the relentless pounding of the wind against them.

Brittni Brinn

Chapter 14
Between Breads

The next morning, Ed woke up sweating, his pale forehead hot to the touch. He retched what little liquid was left in his stomach onto the dirty concrete floor. After wrapping him in her blanket, Pinot gave him the last mouthful of water. She took the plastic bag of pre-made capsules from inside her sweater and gave him two.

"I'll be back soon," she told him. The map marked another supply stop about a two hour's walk north. It could be a dead end, but they were low on food, and Ed wasn't going anywhere. She didn't want to leave him, but he was still lucid enough to take control if Grafters found him in the abandoned garage. "Try to stay awake, okay? It should only be for a few hours." She stood with her pack on her shoulders for what felt like the thousandth time. The bag was mostly empty, but still weighed her down, wanting her to stay with Ed.

He waved weakly, a rivulet of sweat snaking down his face and into the wide cuff of his scarf.

Pinot closed her eyes briefly at the brightness that waited for her outside the garage, shivering as she zipped up her coat. The wind had died down, thankfully, but the still air had had all night to marinate in its own cold. Briskly heading into the wasteland, she swung her arms, bouncing each step to warm her blood as it coursed through her. After a few minutes, the heat reached her cheeks, and she focused on moving forward, her hands stuffed into her pockets.

"Stupid," she mumbled to herself. She'd dragged Ed out here on a stupid whim, and now they were both stuck.

Weak sunlight crossed through the clouds above her, reminding her of the first months after the Event, when the sky was an impenetrable shroud of cotton. She followed the bearing on her compass, lining up the needle with the red arrow pointing north, until she felt the two hours hit their limit. There was a vague lump off to her left; she altered course towards it, her feet numb automatons.

The lump grew and solidified into a row of storefronts. A flower shop, a sandwich place, a second hand store. All connected. A section of street from a quiet tourist town.

There were windows and doors, plenty of places for Grafters to hide. They could have guns, but she doubted if anything short of a shot to the head would take her out for very long. Without Ed, she felt invincible. She was guaranteed old age in a world where people would rarely survive more than a handful of years. Fearless, she stepped onto the sidewalk and turned into the first shop.

The handle was busted; the door easily pushed inward. Inside were bare wire shelves and a center display that had been smashed, exposing the hollow base. The counter was upright, bolted to the floor. No sign of a cash register or debit machine. Underneath were shelves that housed an undisturbed stack of thin sheets of plastic and purple tissue paper. For wrapping flowers, she thought. She lifted the top sheet from the pile and crumpled it in her hand. A cascade of birthdays and Christmases nearly overwhelmed her as she stuffed as much of it into her backpack as she could. Screwed up sheets of tissue paper would serve well as fire starters.

She paused to listen for any sound of movement from the back room. So far, the place seemed deserted.

She nicked a few packs of flower food—for trade, or if she ever needed to start a garden—and a tall tin vase from the corner behind the counter.

The back room was full of dried flowers, some of them covered over with furry white mold. The glass doors to the walk-in fridge had been pulled off their tracks, left off kilter. A coat hung on a hook behind the open back door. A bit big for her, but Ed might need it. She threw it on over her own padded jacket. A black peacoat, with wide square pockets and wooden buttons, more fitted than she felt comfortable wearing on the wasteland. Grafters can't be choosers, she thought, taking on the long-hated name for herself. After all, that's what she'd become. A Grafter.

Something shifted in the front part of the shop. She paused, slowly eased the back screen door open. It creaked a little, but she didn't stop to see if someone followed. She stalked along the back side of the shops, thinking. The sound could've been from something she disturbed during her search. She hooked around the far side of the strip. No sign of anyone out front, only the long stretch of sidewalk and the expanse yawning beyond. She waited. The strip was quiet, and she trusted her instincts. No one had pursued her. Either they were alone and scared, or they were waiting.

She still needed to search the other two shops before returning to Ed. At least one thing they could eat, she decided. Once she found that, she could go.

She checked the secondhand store. Compared to the flower shop, it was surprisingly pristine: the first few rows of hangers were bare, followed by full sections of summer dresses, maternity wear, kids jeans. She found a pair of snow boots in Ed's size, and a crumpled sweater featuring three realistic bats in flight for herself. A couple of toques from a mesh bin, a couple of pens. Her backpack was full to bursting. No sign of food.

A creak drew her attention. Out of the corner of her eye, she saw the change room stall door swing open.

"Who's there?" she asked, calmly. She saw no one, heard nothing except for her heartbeat rising in her ears.

Enough of the secondhand store, she decided.

That left the sandwich shop. *Between Breads* was painted on the front window in flowery letters. The door stuck, and then flew open, setting off a bell overhead. She froze as the bell rang itself out. Pinot quickly scanned the room. Most of the tables were stacked against the far wall, a row of chairs lined up in front of them.

There was one table set with two chairs, next to a low bookcase framing a stack of tattered paperbacks. On the round table was a heavy yellow coffee mug with a thick handle. Pinot walked towards it, intending to pass by in order to scout out the counter and the area beyond. The mug shifted on the table and floated into the air. It tipped slightly, followed by the sound of someone drinking the liquid inside.

Pinot stopped dead. Her brain could not process what was happening and began to tip her into vertigo. She recognized it, the feeling of being in shock. She closed her eyes, focused on slowing her breathing. She heard the mug settle onto the table. When she opened her eyes, the mug was further away from her, as if ready for a person sitting in the far chair.

"I'm sorry," Pinot finally said to the seemingly empty seat, "I didn't know anyone lived here."

A heavy pause. Now that she knew someone was in the room with her, she could sense them, hear their light breathing.

"Sit down, won't you?" came a silver, dangerous voice.

Slipping her backpack onto the floor, Pinot lowered herself into the closest chair. She closed her eyes again, preparing. The chair seat was cushioned, but the back was hard wood. Again she said, "I didn't know."

"I saw everything you took," the voice replied. "It seems there are at least two of you."

The boots, too big for her, the two hats. "I left my friend a little ways back. He's fighting off a fever."

"Clearly he isn't with you."

Pinot nodded. "Oh, can you see me when I–"

"Just because you can't see me, doesn't mean I can't see you."

"Right."

"Are you prepared to pay for what you took?"

"What kind of payment?"

"Well," and Pinot heard the invisible person shift in their chair, "I'm going to need some of your blood."

"My blood."

"Yes."

Pinot considered. "I don't think so."

"I can give you enough food to last you a week," the voice continued, a note of strain underlying their words. "Would that be suitable?"

"How much blood?"

"A pint."

Pinot thought for a moment, then nodded. "That seems like a fair trade."

"Then we're agreed."

The table shook and Pinot felt a pressure across her chest and a pain in her neck. "Don't move now," the voice whispered into her ear, and Pinot closed her eyes and stayed as still as she could, breathing in and out and focusing on that instead of the pressure against her skin, draining her blood.

A fuzziness set in, she fumbled trying to hear her breathing in the dark. "That's enough," she managed, and the pressure released.

Pinot opened her eyes, stars bursting over her vision.

"Here," the voice said, and a hand pressed a piece of cloth to her neck. "I didn't touch the main artery, so the bleeding should stop fairly quickly."

"Thanks for that," Pinot said, taking over. She sat straighter in the chair, breathing deeply and trying to ignore the weakness taking over her body.

"Rest," the voice said, and a drawn woman with warm brown skin and loose black hair sat in the chair across from her. "Drink some of this."

A mug was in Pinot's hand. She sipped it, amazed at the taste of apple juice.

"Finish all of that. I'll get your supplies in order."

Pinot was left alone to drink the rest of the juice. The cut on her neck had already healed over. She felt the room regain its edges, she blinked the spots away.

The woman returned wearing a long-sleeved dress, carrying a plastic bag in one hand and a plate in the other.

"You're a vampire?" Pinot asked her.

The woman laughed quietly. "Not quite. I am very happy to say that I can still enjoy the food of mortals." She set a plate with slices of homemade bread onto the table between them. "No, I don't drink blood to survive. I need it to be seen. The Event was not kind to my genetic code."

"You were invisible because you hadn't had blood..."

"A pint will get me through about a month. By then, I'm perfectly invisible." The woman smiled, her teeth a healthy off-white, a slight gap between the front two. "Let's eat."

They did, Pinot eating the slice of bread slowly. It was fresh, and tasted of rosemary and other savoury herbs that she couldn't name. "Why not stay invisible," she said after a few satisfying bites. "It's the perfect defense against Grafters."

"Many of them avoid this place. They think it's haunted."

"What about people like me who just stumble in?"

"I've handled your kind before."

"I see."

"Some of them are reasonable, like you. Some of them, are not."

"I see."

"You keep saying that."

"Oh, sorry. I'm just trying to understand. But still, why be visible at all?"

The woman's drawn face became even more so. "I'm tired of being invisible."

They finished the bread together, and the woman showed her the contents of the plastic bag. "A loaf of bread, like this one, a couple of cans of fruit, and tea, if you like. I went through all the coffee here long ago."

"Thank you," Pinot said, placing a knowing hand on the woman's shoulder. How long had she been here, alone?

The woman's face eased into a relaxed, warm smile. "Anytime you need supplies, I'm always willing to trade."

"I'll keep that in mind."

Pinot repacked her bag, working in the new supplies: a can of juice in each boot, the loaf of bread filling out the arc at the top of the backpack.

The woman walked Pinot to the door. They looked at each other.

"I should get back to my friend," Pinot said.

The woman kissed her on the cheek. "My name's Irene."

"Pinot."

"Goodbye, Pinot."

"Goodbye."

Brittni Brinn

Chapter 15
Lost Trail

Ed came out of a fever dream, someone's hand on his forehead.

I must've fallen asleep, he mouthed, forgetting that no one could hear him. His eyes flickered open. Pinot was sitting near him, wearing a coat he'd never seen before; it smelled cool, as if the wind had worked its way into the material and was living there. His shoulders and neck ached from falling asleep sitting up, supported by the garage wall.

"I brought back a couple of things," she said, tipping some water to his lips. "Did you take those pills I left?"

He stared at her as the words reached him, and he nodded once. His eyes kept hold of hers, the near black irises reflecting orange from the fire she'd restarted.

"Sleep now." She took off the strange jacket, draped it over him. It made no difference. He couldn't tell if he was too hot or too cold or somewhere in between. A trickle of sweat ran down his spine, between skin and t-shirt. Pinot helped him to lay down.

He thought he slept, though he lived in the flashes of Pinot across the flames, when she leaned near him to wipe the sweat from his forehead.

Minutes, or hours, or days later, he woke up groggy. He could sit up without the room veering sideways. Pinot was sitting next to him, her back against the wall, her eyes closed.

Ed stumbled to the far corner of the room, where they'd set a rusted coffee tin. He nearly missed the opening, but thankfully managed to relieve himself without making too much of a mess. He laughed at himself: even though he and Pinot left the restaurant weeks ago, he was still bashful about bodily functions.

He slowly made his way back to his spot near the fire, sitting closer to Pinot. For warmth he told himself, but when her head found his shoulder he relaxed. A couple of stray snowflakes drifted down from the cracked window overhead. He dozed, still trying to stay aware of any strange sounds above the wind. A door opening or the sound of footsteps…

Pinot stirred about an hour later.

"Shit, why didn't you wake me up? You're the one who should be sleeping."

He placed her hand on his forehead.

"You're right, it's getting better. Still, I'm your doctor, and I want you to be one hundred percent before we go anywhere. Hungry?"

Pinot told him about the invisible woman as she ripped a quarter of the loaf into smaller pieces for them to share. She'd scraped some snow from around the base of the garage outside and melted it in the bottom of the tin vase, adding a tea bag for flavor. She spit in it, to take care of anything malignant in the snow or the years-old tea.

How long have we been here? Ed wrote on a scrap of paper.

"A few days. Your fever broke this morning, I was hoping you'd be okay by tomorrow."

He almost didn't hand her the next piece of paper. *We've probably lost their trail by now.*

Pinot's mouth tightened and she nodded. "It was stupid of me to want to go after them."

No, it made sense.

"I shouldn't have brought you along."

I wanted to come.

Pinot dug her hands into her pockets. "I've been thinking about it, and I don't know what the next move should be. We could stay here, I can get supplies about once a month from Irene. We could go back to the Forager camp, or the restaurant even. Stupid," she muttered to herself now, "Fucking stupid."

Ed nudged her with his elbow, shaking his head. *You're not stupid.*

"I guess I… I wanted to see him. Jax. It's been years, but I think back to what happened with him, and I… I feel sick, even though I know it wasn't my fault. I didn't know that May was making you control him. I—" the bridge of her nose creased in disgust, "I can't imagine how he must've felt. Once he knew. How he must've… hated me. How even now, maybe he thinks back on everything we said to each other, everything we… everything we did, and hates me for it."

We could keep looking.

Pinot's dark gaze rested on the burning wood, the crumbling piece of siding veined with fire. "You should try to sleep. I'll keep lookout for a while."

Ed tucked his pen and paper into his pocket.

Brittni Brinn

Chapter 16
Decision

Pinot climbed over the knee-high snow drifts that had collected around the detached garage. Emptying the tin of waste a few metres behind the building, she squinted against the sunlight reflecting off the crystalized surface of the wasteland. They had to decide today. One more snowfall, and they'd be stuck for the rest of the winter.

Precipitation was still a puzzle. No constant patterns, no idea of what time of day it'd most likely snow, how many times. The atmosphere had been fucked over and was now trying to get itself un-fucked. Pinot knew what that was like. It took time.

Pinot pulled the side door shut behind her, locked the deadbolt. Ed huddled in the corner, extra coats and blankets piled on top of him. A couple days before, she'd brought a tarp back from the secondhand store, hung it from the ceiling to insulate their corner. They decided that during the day, they'd try to avoid fires. The garage siding wouldn't last forever, and nights were colder by far. Despite her efforts, Ed's fever was creeping back, not quite eradicated, a deep cough developing in his chest.

"Stupid," she tortured herself again. This was her fault. Maybe nothing else was, but keeping Ed here was something she could fix.

But she'd seen the glimmer of bronze in the distance,

believed that the SUs couldn't be that far off, that she could catch up.

The light in the garage door motor flickered on. Ed must be awake under there, trying to get her attention.

"Yeah?" she said, replacing the coffee tin on the rust ring staining the concrete.

The light flickered on again.

"What?" she snapped.

No response. The pile of cloth was still, and the light stayed off.

Pinot felt a sick jab of guilt. She half-ran over to him. "Ed, I'm here. Did you need something?" And her hands in her fingerless gloves peeled back the clothes and blankets, desperate for him to be joking.

His eyes were closed, his cheeks pale, his red-brown beard tangled with his scarf. His breathing shallow.

"Hey. Hey!"

Ed's eyes flickered open, a brief flash of light.

"Shit." The fever was back in full force. It had been decided for her. They'd spend the rest of the winter in the garage.

Chapter 17
Irene's

It was Pinot's third time back to Irene's.

"How's your friend Ed doing?" she asked, raising her mug of tea to her lips.

Pinot wiped the last of the blood from the closing wound on her neck. "Still weak. Sleeps most of the day."

"I can give you some extra food this time."

Pinot held up her hands. "I can't, you need it."

"Yes, I suppose that's true." Irene's green eyes took on a faraway look. "If you do end up leaving at the end of the winter, I'll have to find a new trading partner."

Pinot took a sip from her mug, savoring the fruit punch. "You could come with us."

"This is my home."

"I can understand that."

"Is that where you're going? Home?"

Pinot laughed shortly. "Can't go back there."

"Why not?"

"I don't think the person who runs the place would approve. She thinks I did something...rash."

"Did you?"

Pinot was caught in the woman's question, swirling deep in her eyes. "Yeah, I guess. I... There was this Grafter. He was going to kill May's baby. So I killed him."

"That sounds perfectly reasonable to me."

"But I didn't just kill him, Irene. I…cut him open. I was… upset because I had this patient."

At 'patient', Irene placed both hands on the table, triumphantly. "I knew it."

Pinot stopped mid-sip, realizing her mistake.

"I always thought there was something special about your blood. I haven't had any stomachaches since the first time we met. The Event did something to you as well."

"Think of it as a bonus." Pinot set her empty mug on the table.

"You had a patient?" Irene moved her chair closer to Pinot's.

"He was dying. Bladder cancer. I wanted to try surgery, but I had no idea what to look for, how to keep the blood loss at a minimum. It was…frustrating, not being able to do anything for him. When I killed the Grafter…I thought that by going through his abdomen, I could find something that would help. But only for a moment. I knew it was hopeless. So I chose to enjoy it instead."

"The leader thought you had overdone it. Killing him."

"Yes and no. I think she understood why I killed him, just not what happened afterward. She called me an animal, and that's fair. It's what I am."

Irene's slender hands gently lifted Pinot's fist from the table and held it. "I've seen a lot of people pass through here. Some of them are desperate, some of them are cruel, that's true. But you're not like that. Not at all."

The final pull of Irene's eyes was too much for Pinot. She placed a hand on Irene's cheek and Irene didn't push it away. They kissed.

Pinot threaded her fingers into Irene's hair as she felt Irene's hands reach up under her jacket for her waist.

"I don't want to be invisible," Irene sighed into her ear.

Chapter 18
In the Garage

Ed pictured the window in the dining room, his padded chair pulled up close to the glass. It was so early that everyone was still asleep. He liked to sit here, sometimes, in the quiet before the restaurant filled with people. Outside, the forest was a dim silhouette, grey lines and navy greens crossing over and over, a chaotic lattice that was also harmonious. So many trees, branching into hundreds of outcomes: fruitful possibilities or deadwood, sunlight, rot, chloro-filled contentment or breaking off, falling away.

Ed thought about these outcomes, his focus moving inward to the window itself. The heat inside and the cold out there created a film of condensation. He traced after a drop as it ran into others, each new drop pulling it from its earlier path in quick diagonals, the drop growing heavier and heavier as it rushed to the end of the glass. The trees, the water drops. That's when he got the idea.

I remember them from when I was young, he told Pinot. She was reclining next to him by the fire, feeding it a shard of siding. *Did you ever play text adventure games?*

She shook her head, keeping an eye on the split wood. She relaxed slightly as it drew flames into itself and started to burn.

They're also called Interactive Fiction. You usually wake up or find yourself in a strange room. Then you solve puzzles to progress the story.

You can pick up objects, fight monsters. But it's all based on text commands you type into the computer. You have to imagine what happens.

"So you decided to make one."

Ed nodded, touching the nib of the pen to his tongue. The ink was running out. He'd have to switch to one of the back-up pens sooner than he'd thought. *I knew I could set up an elementary OS for the computers Arissa had in storage. And I did, and then I started making the game.* After a moment, he decided to write the next line. *You never played it.*

Pinot shrugged, "I guess I was busy with other things."

We have all the time in the world now.

***

Pinot was reading through *The Catcher in the Rye* for the millionth time. Occasionally, Ed would read some of it, but he was more interested in writing notes to himself accompanied by narrative trees. Levels for his video game, he would explain, making adjustments as Pinot gave feedback.

It was all about passing the time, about focusing on something other than how cold they were, or how hungry the daytime hours could be.

Once a day, Pinot would get them up and they would walk around the garage, stretching out their bodies, doing push-ups if they felt like it. And then they would lean against each other until the room turned grey, and they could start the fire.

They'd found a dust-caked jar of colorful Canadian Tire money on one of the shelves bolted to the side wall. Pinot fished out some of the paper bills, screwed them into a long twist of paper. She used it as a taper, carrying fire from the candle they kept lit during the day to the small offering of firewood, lighting the last of the tissue paper, hoping to God that the kindling would catch.

"It should be the last trip," Pinot said, holding her palms out to catch the warmth. "I'll go tomorrow, pick up some supplies. Then we can plan our route."

Ed shuffled closer to the fire, the black coat draped over his shoulders. His fingers went for pen and paper.

We don't have to go back.

Pinot sucked air through her teeth. "No, we should. You're in no condition to rough it." And this puzzled Pinot, because the pills he was taking, the spit she added to their water without fail, it should've been more than enough to heal Ed. But somehow the cough hung on, and the occasional onset of sweat flushed his brow. "I'll ask Irene for a little extra for the trip, but I may have to stay later than usual."

With a small smile, Ed nodded. *I know.*

"So I'll go tomorrow. And if it turns out–"

That's when they both heard it. The rattling of the garage door, and then someone trying the door handle.

Ed and Pinot froze. The handle went still, but someone was outside. They waited it out, knowing that if the person was alone, it'd be unlikely they'd try to break in. Ed's mind was already in the garage mechanism, in case they short fused the key code panel from the outside.

Pinot's mind raced. The person outside must've seen the orange glow of their fire through the upper window. They knew that someone was inside. What were they waiting for?

Stakeout. Ed handed her the message, and she suspected he was right.

"Boost me?" she whispered. Ed staggered up, bracing his back against the wall. She stepped in his cupped hands, planted her other foot on his shoulder. They'd both lost so much weight, she was sure the bones in her feet were digging in as painfully as his shoulder dug up into her soles. She gripped the windowsill, squinted down through the cracked window. She didn't see anyone, no footprints in the weak arc of light cast down onto the snow.

She scrambled off Ed's shoulder. "Two hour watches," she whispered to him, "I'll start."

For the first time in a while, Pinot flipped open her switchblade.

Brittni Brinn

Chapter 19
Ed's Dream

Ed and the dungeon wraith were in the mountains. Hiking up a gravel road, the incline cutting through the trees. A chill alpine wind pulled at his hair. The dungeon wraith was always a few metres ahead, a translucent grey shadow. Occasionally, it turned back to wait for him, its eyes flashing like red stars. Once past the treeline, the terrain became rocky, vegetation diminishing to ground creepers and lichens. The sky pale, closer to white than blue.

"I've been here before," he thought, but couldn't remember when. He paused and turned to look down into the forest they'd just travelled through. As he turned, the incline shifted around him and suddenly he was standing on a flat rocky desert, looking up into the forest as it extended before him in an endless slope, curving slightly at the horizon.

His nausea settled, his body adjusted to the vertigo. Up and down had changed, and he wasn't sure if he should turn around, or hike upwards into the forest.

The dungeon wraith, he could sense it hovering just behind his right shoulder.

"We should go," it whispered, and encompassed him in a cloud of fog and fire that consumed him until they both faded away into ash.

Brittni Brinn

Chapter 20
My Hero

Pinot put off her supply run for another two days.

We haven't seen anyone, Ed wrote, *maybe they were just looking for a place to sleep. When they noticed the firelight, they got scared off.*

Something wasn't right about it, Pinot decided. But she didn't have much of a choice. They were out of food, and if they were going to make it to Summerland, they had to build up Ed's strength.

"Okay, I'm going. But I swear I'll be back before dark."

She left him her switchblade, even though she knew he didn't need it.

"See you soon." She gripped his hand, gave him a rare smile. The fever was gone from his eyes, leaving them puffy and red. He smiled back at her through his beard.

Pinot opened the side door, Ed followed to lock it behind her. Their eyes met through the closing door and Ed winked. It surprised her, and she laughed. The warmth of the laugh kept the cold from crawling inside her as she walked into the wasteland, watching for anyone staking out their hideout. She saw no one.

***

"Irene?" Pinot asked the air once the bell over the door had settled.

"Dammit!"

Pinot followed the swearing into the back room, stopping in the doorway.

"I didn't think you were coming." Irene's silver voice came from the blanket-covered pallet she used as a bed. "When I heard the bell, I guess I got a little excited, and rolled my ankle. I think I sprained it."

Pinot sat tentatively on the edge of the bed, following Irene's invisible touch as it guided her down.

"I can help," Pinot said. "But I need to see it first." Pinot braced herself as she felt the still-strange pressure across her collarbones, the suction on her neck. Irene began to appear, her lips then her curved nose, green eyes, her full hairline, strands of black hair all the way down to their split ends. Her chin and neck became visible next, the rest of her washing into color.

Pinot waited for the dizziness to pass. Irene kept her hand compressed over the wound as it healed. "Let's take a look," Pinot said after a moment and kissed Irene a quick hello.

The ankle was starting to swell. Pinot felt the joint, she didn't find any broken bones. "Mild sprain," Pinot concluded, emphasizing 'mild.' "Keep it elevated. If you have anything I could use as bandages, I can wrap it for you."

"My hero, the doctor." Irene pulled Pinot close for another kiss.

***

Pinot scooped snow from outside the shop, keeping an eye out for Grafters. A light snowfall drew down a gauzy blind, softening the wasteland. She thought of Ed, hoping he was okay. Of course he was. The person who had tried to get into the garage had doubtlessly moved on, found their own shelter. There was no reason for them to return to a tiny run-down building in the middle of nowhere. Pinot sealed the snow in a sandwich bag and took it to Irene.

"You should rest." Pinot sat next to her on the pallet.

"So should you."

Pinot climbed over Irene and helped her set her foot up on a pillow. She made a depression for the bag of snow to sit in, half-over Irene's swelling ankle. Then she settled on her side and told Irene about the mysterious handle rattling in the night, their plans for leaving the garage.

"It must've been hard for you to come here, when you knew it could be dangerous for Ed."

"Ed knows how to take care of himself. Like you."

"Apparently not," Irene laughed, pointing at her foot.

"I should really get back to him."

Irene placed a hand on Pinot's waist. "Yes, I suppose you should. You're going to need supplies."

Pinot had never seen where Irene kept her food stores. "I can carry you wherever you need."

"No need to be dramatic," Irene smiled. "Just give me a few minutes."

***

Pinot woke up, her arm draped over Irene's stomach. From how thirsty she was, she'd been asleep a couple of hours, at least. The plastic bag next to Irene's ankle was fat with water.

Pinot climbed over her, turned the corner into the front room of the store, and found herself faced with a black sky pouring a blizzard over the wasteland. There would be no going back tonight. "Fuck," she mumbled, bracing her hand against the ice-cold countertop.

Wanting to be here. Wanting to be with Ed. Hungry all over.

Brittni Brinn

Chapter 21
Fog

Ed was woken up by someone shaking the door handle. It was light out, and the howling wind had moved off, taking the ice and snowfall along with it. Pinot still hadn't returned; he hoped that she'd spent the night with Irene, didn't get caught in the storm.

The door handle rattled again. There were voices. Muffled by the walls, but he could make out two of them at least, one of them approaching from far away. It sounded like Pinot, shouting at whoever was outside the door. He could make out the response, a "Don't come any closer!" before that voice moved off towards the voice that sounded like Pinot.

Ed was frozen, uncertain of how to proceed. Should he wait for Pinot to deal with the other voice? Her knife was folded up, useless, in his hand. Should he go out there and try to help her? He closed his eyes searching for an outlet, for a strange brain to sieve into, but there was only fog. He couldn't keep the search up for long. He felt short-circuited, like there was a loose wire somewhere in his mind, draining power.

The voices were shouting, he couldn't make out the words. Right as he stood, he heard a gunshot.

And then he was running. Unfastening the door, wrenching it open, stumbling into the snow-bright outdoors. His hands lifted to shield his eyes, trying to see through the gaps in his fingers. He could make out a woman, but it wasn't Pinot. She turned to face him, her grin marred by missing teeth.

His eyes adjusted now, Ed frantically searched for Pinot, but everywhere he looked there was only un-bloodied snow. He looked to the woman, who was still grinning at him. Her grin was suddenly swallowed up as her mouth opened wide like an air horn, the sound of a gunshot echoing from inside. Then, the lips formed another shape, a sharp frown, and a mumbling issued from her, an exact copy of Pinot's voice as if heard through a wall.

Ed understood then. He didn't try to resist. He'd left the door wide open in his hurry to save Pinot. The fog in his brain had sieved down into the rest of his body. He could sense the darkness about to envelop him, how he'd soon be turned into a dungeon wraith. One last try at reaching into the woman's mind, but the fog was too thick, something was preventing him. Footsteps behind him in the snow. A set of hands closed around his neck, and the fog swallowed him.

Chapter 22
Erased

The garage was looted when Pinot returned. Neatly picked through, the tarp cut down, their extra clothes swiped from the floor. No blood. It gave Pinot hope that Ed was merely missing or was circling back to the garage after an attack.

There were scattered footprints in the snow, two sets, and a third she recognized as Ed's. The wind had erased their trail, which ended about five metres out from the garage.

She locked the door behind her and sat against it. At first, she stayed alert, sensing every sound, every shift in air, trying to determine if anyone else was in the garage with her. Meeting Irene had shown her that everything was possible in the post-Event world. Not sensing anything, her eyes drifted over to the bare corner where she and Ed had spent the winter, meagerly surviving. Sleeping next to each other. Telling each other about their first kiss, what they had wanted to be when they were kids, the worst thing they had ever done. The person they missed the most.

She had to leave, right now. The people who made the other two sets of footprints, they'd staked out the garage. They knew that someone was coming back. They could be watching her right at this very moment.

Pinot breathed deeply through her nose, pressing the tears from her eyes with the rough heels of her hands. She braced herself against the door and stood. The corner, the charred remains of the campfire, caught at her. Held her.

She crouched down facing the wall she and Ed had shared during so many sleepless nights. If only she had her knife. She picked a stray pen lid off the ground, all that she had left of him.

Using the nub, she scratched a word into the paint. Pocketed the pen lid. Took one last look around.

She closed the side door on her way out. No way to lock it. They never had a key.

If Ed was out there, he'd make it back here one day. If he made it this far, maybe he'd sit next to their fire and wonder what had happened to her. And then he'd see the word scratched into the wall. And it would tell him what no other Grafter in this wasteland could understand. Where she was going. Where they'd see each other again. At least, that was what she wanted to believe.

Book Four

Part Four

Chapter 1
Gardening

Fitting the groove in her boot over the heavy line of the shovelhead, Arissa pressed it into the earth. They were almost done turning the soil, making a garden bed for the seeds Milo had brought with him. There were tomatoes, lettuce, carrot seeds. She thought of what fresh vegetables would mean to their community. Theodore had gotten them through the winter, but she wasn't sure his ability to duplicate objects—and food—would hold out for another year.

Why? she wondered for the thousandth time. Why were they losing them? The gifts that had come in wake of the Event, why were they fading away?

It had been a hard winter. They had lost some people, gained a few new ones. In the months since Pinot had killed the Grafter, Arissa had started a new schedule. Not for kitchen volunteers or maintenance work. For lookouts. For security. Stef and Markus fell easily into these roles. It was as if they had been reserving themselves for this kind of work, something they knew the ins and outs of. The waiting. The late nights patrolling through the woods. When they first came to the restaurant, they had been reserved and scared; Nick had helped them open up, start to live again. This was their home now. And they wanted to protect it.

Arissa nodded to them as they followed the worn clay trail

into the acre of trees. Stef was short, barely five feet, with brittle mousy hair and an off-set nose. Markus was built thin, wiry, with brown hair so light it was almost grey. They wore their jackets unzipped; spring was just starting to turn warm.

A hand gently squeezed her shoulder. "My turn." It was Victoria, her other hand supporting Lucas, who was straining towards a grey squirrel chattering from a tree branch. "I hope you don't mind taking over babysitting for me?"

Arissa said "Not at all" and gave her the shovel, taking Lucas as she went.

"What is this squirrel up to, Lucas, hmm?" Arissa asked him as they both observed. The squirrel darted between two branches, as if looking for something. "Trying to find their friend?"

Lucas watched the squirrel, a solemn concentration pervading his face, his bright, bronze-shot eyes invested in the animal's every movement.

Arissa turned her attention to the garden plot as the last of the dirt was turned over, from dry to damp, from dead leaves and rusted pine needles to dark peat and insects and petrified wood chips. Each person left furrows as they went—she thought of foreheads, ready for ideas to be planted, and then to grow. She also thought of orchards, vast rows of trees with branches to be cut, to be grafted, to bind and heal.

She could tell from the way everyone stood, hands on their still shovels, their voices joined in conversation, that they had completed the work. The garden was ready.

"Time to go in!" she called, to regain Lucas' attention, but also to let the weary backs and shoulders and hands know that they had done well, and now it was time to rest.

Chapter 2
A Message

May stretched her arms overhead, listing to the side to ease the cramp in her back. She'd been digging since lunchtime, and the smell of dirt was tickling the inside of her nose. She was certain that the pits of her sweater were soaked in sweat. Despite all of these things—or, in fact because of them—she felt incredible. Hungry, yes. Tired, absolutely. But look at that garden, all ready for greens and veggies and maybe some flowers. A feeling similar to completing a painting or walking through an exhibit she had helped to organize filled her.

"Good work today!" she called to Sophie. The older woman was collecting shovels in her patient way, her grey braids tied up in an old scarf. Sophie grinned and lifted a hand. Rhonda was helping to load the shovels into a wheelbarrow, which they'd take around back and lock in the shed.

May whistled an old pop song as she made her way to the stream. She scrubbed her hands, loosening the dirt under her fingernails, splashing her face for good measure. She was on kitchen duty and didn't want to get dirt in the soup.

Arissa came up next to her, rinsing her hands and dabbing some of the cool water on the back of her neck.

"Victoria said you were taking care of Lucas," May said, noticing that her son wasn't with Arissa.

"Nick's got him, don't you worry," she smiled. "Didn't want

you to be the only one in the kitchen."

May relaxed. "I can handle it."

"Not the seasoning you can't."

"That was one time!"

"You thought the cinnamon was chili powder—"

"Like I said, one time—"

"It was among the worst things I've ever tasted!"

May splashed some water at her, laughing.

Arissa laughed with her until something across the stream caught her attention. She stood up slowly, her whole body suddenly tense.

May mirrored her movements. There had been wolf sightings over the winter, and just last week Rhonda had spotted a bear moving through the woods. She followed Arissa's sightline, straightening up, her hands ready in front of her.

But it wasn't a wolf, or a bear.

It was a woman, her face half covered in an old scar, half obscured by a shock of white hair.

It was Pinot.

Her clothes were tattered and twisted, dirty beyond belief, old mud splashes and streaks of dirt dying the front of her clothes a burnt-out grey. She didn't say anything, only stared into the stream as it tumbled through its channel.

"Where's Ed?" Arissa asked her in a flat voice.

"I'm not staying," Pinot said, ignoring the question. "I only came to leave a message."

Arissa pressed her lips together, her eyes narrowed. Her question hung in the air.

"When Ed gets here, tell him not to look for me. That's all." Pinot watched the stream a moment longer. A shiver went through her, and she turned to go.

May watched it all as if from far away. Flashes of the Grafter with the gun cut through her mind, sharp jabs of fear as she saw him leering over Lucas. The moment Pinot had caught Lucas and returned him, safe and sound. May had never gotten a chance to tell Pinot that she was grateful. That she was sorry.

When May saw that Pinot was leaving, she snapped back into her body. She summoned a simple phrase before it was too late. "We miss you," she said, sending her words over the water between them.

Maybe Pinot heard, maybe she didn't. She pushed a tree branch up as she passed underneath it, her body clearly malnourished. The tree trunks obscured her from view as she moved further into the forest.

"May," Arissa's voice was angry now. "Keep this to yourself, please. Pinot abandoned us long ago. There's no need to drag everyone through that again. Especially not Rhonda."

May undid the elastic tying up her hair and combed the strands into a tighter ponytail. "I only told her the truth. You miss her more than anyone."

They rinsed their hands in the stream once more, and walked back up the hill to the restaurant.

Brittni Brinn

Chapter 3
Argument

That night, May lifted her head off the pillow to find Isak sitting at the end of their bed. "You're back," she said, though she knew that for him it felt as if no time had passed. She apprehended his question, the one he always asked. "About 8 hours."

Isak sighed and climbed up the length of the bed, settling onto his side. "How was Lucas today?"

She brushed Isak's hair from off his forehead and forced a smile. "He had a busy afternoon, fell asleep as soon as I put him to bed." They glanced over at the crib, listening over the sound of their own breathing for his, a whisper of rhythm. Satisfied that he was asleep, they relaxed.

"Sorry."

"It's okay," May smiled, for real this time. She knew Isak tried not to skip forward on purpose, and lately, his cases of time travel had been rare.

Pressing a kiss on her cheek, Isak pushed himself to standing. He grunted a little as his legs took his body weight, and then made his way to Lucas's crib. "Hey little guy. Sorry I missed your day," he said, leaning forward.

"Let him sleep," May said softly.

But Isak reached for the little heap of human, lifting Lucas into his bare arms.

May strained against the urge to rush over and pull Lucas away. Instead, she gritted her teeth. "I wish you wouldn't."

"He's my son too," Isak replied, matter-of-fact.

It was their only argument. If Isak should hold the baby. Because if something pulled him strongly enough, if he skipped forward, the secure ring of his arms would be gone.

"I'm not going anywhere," he cooed to their child, rocking him gently.

May tried to relax, propping a pillow behind her back. It was nighttime, but hard to tell when. Unlike the rooms on the other side of the lower level, theirs didn't have a window. She watched the dim figure of her husband until he finally replaced Lucas in the safety of the crib.

"There," Isak turned to her, "Perfectly safe." She could feel the sharpness in his voice.

This time, May thought to herself, but it only takes one slip up. Outwardly, she sighed in acceptance and welcomed Isak back into bed.

Chapter 4
Rhonda

Rhonda found her way through the trees behind the restaurant. Each branch cut across her vision as if backlit or outlined in solid fire. The world had become more well-defined since Milo's death. She could place her hand against the trunk of one of these lodgepole pines and sense each overlap of bark, the sticky residue of sap, and come away with it imprinted into her mind as well as her hand. The smell, too, was more present to her as spring loosened the soil. Clearer, more painful. The sudden call of a bird nearly brought her to tears.

As she reached the small row of graves, her eyes completely dried. She found Milo's namestone, the fourth in line. The flowers she'd scattered were melding into the earth, nibbled at by rabbits. She smiled a little, thinking of how Milo used to chase rabbits away from their garden, flapping his old coat to scare them off.

If only they'd stayed there. Not just the place, but in that piece of time where they'd lived peacefully in that broken school building.

Her hand went to his watch on her left wrist, pressing its cool glass face into her palm. "I'm still angry at you," she told him. Even so, she was grateful she hadn't had to bury him alone.

Not sure where she would go, she continued walking past the graves. Sunlight edged in through the layers of leaves and branches. She took in the rustling of the woods, the occasional buzz of insects. A small skunk crossed the path in front of her, rooting around in the leaves.

She was on the other side of the restaurant now, the thickly grown hillside that sloped down towards the distant highway. The ridge was there, a couple of feet below.

Settling onto the packed earth and tightly wound moss, she let her legs hang over the edge. The hill continued its descent around her, only the ridge resisting the flow of the woods and the impetus of gravity. Rhonda dropped a pinecone between her feet, down into the brush, listening as it tumbled unseen through the undergrowth.

She asked herself, as she had many times in the past couple of months, if she should stay at the restaurant. It's what Milo had wanted for her. And it felt good to be with people, to have their presence around her as she slept. She didn't worry so much about Grafters breaking in anymore. Everybody took care of each other. It was the only thing they could do.

She heard branches cracking, the bright sound of someone coming through the woods behind her. "Thought I'd find you out here." Nick sat down next to her and crossed his legs.

Rhonda didn't say anything. She leaned into him, their shoulders matching. She could still leave. But right now, all she wanted was to sit next to Nick and listen to the forest. They watched the tops of the trees until they got hungry, and then, together, they walked up the hill and went in.

Chapter 5
On Edge

What happens next?
How the fuck am I supposed to know?

Jeff read the message onscreen and swiped it away. They'd been waiting for Jax to appear for the past hour, and both of them were getting anxious.

Jeff thought of Caden, sitting in a chair identical to his in the other SU, worrying his lip with his teeth or cracking his knuckles. They'd had time to learn each other's habits by now, spent enough nights together, video called if the trip got long or boring.

During their journey, Jeff had matched his treadmill settings to the SU's progress, running for twenty minutes then spending the rest of the day in his own sweat. Couldn't burn too many calories, but he wanted to stay in shape. Something could happen. The SU could break down (unlikely) or they'd have to fight off Grafters (more likely). The worst scenario he could imagine would be if Caden kicked him out: he'd be left stranded, alone on the wasteland with his bike. They were far beyond familiar territory. He wouldn't know where to go.

Sorry, Caden's message appeared on the screen in front of him, *I'm on edge.*

Jeff knew the feeling. *We should be careful.* He sensed in his gut that this meeting was not going to go well. How did they know they could trust Jax anyway? Just because he led them here, told them how the SUs worked? He promised them a better life and on top of that, the security of numbers. A whole colony of people living in SUs. That was better than trying to scrounge a living on the wasteland. But it could be a lie. It could be a trap.

Jeff glanced up at the screen monitoring the edge of the drop-off, about 10 metres ahead of them. Jax had instructed them to wait, and not to get too close. Unsteady, he claimed. Despite the impressive resolution of the SU's cameras, Jeff couldn't make anything out past the ragged horizon of land. Only sky, pale blue, rosy clouds streaking across, a high wind carving them into tattered faces, shifting swirls.

Here he comes. Caden's message went unanswered—Jeff had already noticed the bronze dome as it nudged into frame, coming at them from the right. Jeff swung in his chair and pulled the ladder away from the wall, setting it up for a quick exit. He wanted to have a way out. After all, now that they were in the neighbourhood, Jax might be able to regain control of the SUs.

He turned the padded chair back to face the wall of screens. Watched the bronze dome with its hundred glowing sensors as it inched towards them.

Chapter 6
Stable One

Along with Lucas's birth came a new tension. A small hand reaching, a mouth hungry and crying. The need to protect it; the fear of failing. May could sense it in herself, how strained she had become between the two. Only Isak cut through these feelings, sometimes as a kind word, sometimes as an absence. He could be next to her, then on the other side of time in the blink of an eye.

So she was the stable one. She was the one picking Lucas up in the middle of the night. She was the one he could depend on.

Isak laughed with Lucas. They played games on the patch of floor in their private room – once a storage closet. Isak told poems, stories, by rote, or as close as he could come. They had no more books. They'd all been burned away, under pots and pans, on the worst and coldest nights. But he remembered enough. And one day Lucas would be old enough to learn.

May held Lucas. When he tripped, when he fell on his face as small children do, she was the one to hold him. Who knew if Isak would be there. Who knew when he would return.

Their only argument often went this way: Isak would swing Lucas by his hands, or rock him back and forth as part of a game, and May would say "I wish you wouldn't."

Isak would smile, but the bronze crack in his dark eyes would flash and he would say "He's my son too. He's my son."

And then one day, it happened.

Isak was holding Lucas as their son climbed up on one of the chairs in the dining room. Helping him along, lifting just enough of the child's weight to make it seem that Lucas was doing everything on his own. Lucas had grown out of the spaceship patterned jumper months before. Arissa had traded some pasta for a small t-shirt one of the caravans brought through. The pale purple hem of the shirt reached his round knees, covering the cloth diaper he wore underneath. May was embarrassed that they couldn't do better for him, but nobody, especially Lucas, thought worse of her for it.

Isak was lifting Lucas. And just as Lucas crested the table, May noticed a tightening in Isak's jaw that she had come to recognize. A stoic response to some deep desire. He was fighting off the pull, the inevitable draw into the future.

She saw it all in a second, but before she could reach Lucas, it happened. Isak disappeared.

"Lucas?"

Where the small figure of her son had been was an empty space. Had he fallen off the table, behind the chair? Had he lost his balance when Isak disappeared? She crouched down, gripping the tabletop with her fingers.

"Lucas, where did you go? Sweetheart?"

A deep spike of nausea pierced her stomach.

There was no sign of her son. There was no sign of her husband.

Both of them had disappeared.

Chapter 7
Tinged Red

Caden followed the approaching SU's progress onscreen. It stopped a few feet away from them. After a few minutes, a young man climbed out from the hatch. He was thin, his body all angles under the grungy sleeveless shirt and floral swim shorts. A pair of silver wires looped over each shoulder, each tinged red in the sunset glow cutting along the ridge. He looked up at them, smiling widely so his sharpened eye teeth also caught the light.

"You've come a long way, so far, so far. Come on out, have a chat with Jax-y boy."

Caden didn't like this. He'd gotten used to living in the armoured apartment— it was safe and smelled familiar. He wasn't a hardened Grafter like Jeff. This place was part of him now, not something he could just leave. All the same, he put a cheerful face on it.

"Just a minute!" he said, and then sat back from the screens. On the open chat box to his left, he typed, *What do you think?* to Jeff, who immediately responded *No*.

"Actually, Jax, why don't we talk like this for a while? It's been a long trip like you said, and I'm feeling a little worn out."

It seemed impossible, but Jax's grin grew even wider. "I understand, I understand. Made the trip myself a few years ago. Gets boring in there, doesn't it?"

"We managed okay, I think," Caden replied. A message from Jeff popped up on the other screen: *We need to see if he's telling the truth.*

"Where are the others?" Caden asked as casually as he could, "You mentioned there would be a colony or something?"

"Oh, you'll see. They're all so excited to meet you. It's been a long time since we've had anybody new. We usually don't trust new people, you see. Got betrayed a while back. Jax learned his lesson."

Talking in third person, Caden typed, *super creepy.* "So," he stated, deciding on a different tactic, "how'd you come across these Survival Units?"

"A story!" Jax laughed, "You want a story?" And he settled in front of them, as if the three of them were old friends sitting around a campfire. He held up his hands, parallel to each other, bringing them into a particular slice of time. He took a deep breath, his nostrils flared, and he began. "So there's this guy. Jax. And he's a punk, right? Like, mohawk haircut and everything. And he was part of this gang, the Opaldines? Really cutthroat kind of crew. Jax got bloody running with them. Anyway, his parents were scientists, and invented these Survival Units. Jax was already gone by then, but he knew about them. Then, the Event happened. The rest of his gang were fucking killed. When he was wandering around the wasteland, he ran into a group of SUs. What else could he do? He joined them."

"And you've been out here ever since? What about our SUs, why were they left—"

"Shh, shh, I'm not there yet." Jax took another deep breath, crossing his arms over his chest. "So Jax joined them. He was their leader. He led them west, further and further away from the dead city. They took supplies from the patches they came across. One was a convenience store, and that's where Jax found the murderer and her twisted crew of mutants, and they said, *please, please bring us with you,* and Jax was a good leader so he said, *yes, you can come along.* But the mutants had a way to control Jax, they got into his head and the murderer seduced him—"

We have to go. Jeff's message cut through Jax's monotone, and Caden typed back *Yes please.* This guy was clearly unstable, and Caden was getting the warning buzz in the back of his head, the response that had saved him from many unsavory situations in the past.

He pressed the wheel button on the grid in front of him, the one that should've opened the navigation screen. Nothing changed. The screen remained fixed on Jax, who was standing now and pacing as he continued his story, his voice becoming louder and sharper until he stopped dead and looked straight at them.

"Jax knew it was the only way to keep them safe. So he put them to sleep, at the bottom of the ocean…"

Controls are locked, Jeff typed, and in a panic Caden pulled the ladder from the wall. He jumped to the top step and tried the hatch. The mechanism was jammed, he couldn't push hard enough to dislodge it.

"You've probably tried to leave by now," Jax's sharp voice announced as Caden rammed his shoulder, painfully, up into the hatch. "So wonderful of you to bring these extra SUs here for me. Really, I thank you both."

Caden staggered down, and fell into the padded chair, his head suddenly feeling too big for his body. The air in his throat, in his lungs, began to burn. On the screen, the small figure that was Jax was standing still, an arrogant throw in his shoulders. His smile less manic, and more deadly.

"I've thought about adding you to the group, but you've been rude and tried to leave during my story, a story I told from the heart," and he hit himself twice on the chest with his fist. "Can't trust outsiders," he said, "I've learned my lesson."

Caden tried to type, to tell Jeff to get out of there, but the words came out funny. His hands felt as if each finger was filled with sand. His head listed forward, the screens crossed into each other, the bright menu grid cutting the image of Jax's grinning face into hundreds of tiny repeating squares. And then, a heavy quilt of darkness.

Brittni Brinn

Chapter 8
Where Do We Go From Here?

May paced the kitchen, Arissa leaning against the industrial dishwasher across from her.

"They'll be back."

"Oh, I know, I know," May muttered, stopping for a moment to wipe a puddle of water from the island's marble countertop. "How could I have been so careless?"

"You didn't know this would happen," Arissa noted, shifting her weight to her other hip.

"If I had, Isak would never have been allowed to touch him!"

Arissa remained silent, tracking May as she moved back and forth along the counter.

"I don't mean that." May stopped, crossing her arms. "At least, I don't want to mean it. But what am I going to say when he just pops back in wherever he pleases? He won't even know that he took Lucas with him."

"You'll have to tell him."

May released her arms with an angry sigh. "Then he'll feel bad, you know Isak. He'll feel guilty and try to make it better. Then he'll get frustrated and skip ahead. Like he always does."

"You can't control his behavior," Arissa cautioned. "Just like he shouldn't control yours. You have to trust that he can handle this. Just be patient."

"Easy for you to say, you don't have any kids." May closed her eyes, swaying as if a wave had washed over her. She looked over the kitchen island at Arissa. "I'm sorry. I didn't know that would hurt you so much."

Arissa cleared her throat. "Keep going."

"I only meant that if Isak can bring things with him, into the future, he's going to have to keep better control of himself."

"Has he ever brought you with him?"

May considered this for a moment. "He's skipped ahead while touching me, but I've never gone with him as far as I know. I always have to pass the time normally to catch up."

"Maybe there's a reason Isak can bring Lucas with him. Maybe Lucas has a gift."

"I...I hadn't thought of that."

"We won't know anything for sure until they're back. May," Arissa was as serious as May had ever seen her, "this isn't going to be easy. But you and Isak are going to figure it out."

May nodded, but her face contracted. "What's going to happen to Lucas?"

Arissa opened her arms. May returned her hug and they stood in the dark kitchen, waiting.

Chapter 9
The End of the World

Jeff sat near the edge of the drop off, gazing into the darkness. The stars, he knew, were up there, but he was dizzy and couldn't keep his head set right. He dropped his chin to his chest, taking deep breaths. Occasionally, he hung his head to the side and retched foul-smelling saliva onto the sand. It was sand, he hadn't noticed while he was in the SU. Maybe this whole ridge was part of some vast desert. The night air was cold, really cold. It bore into his clothes, humidity seeping into his bones. He wished for another coat. There was a swishing sound he couldn't quite place, maybe the wind, blowing back and forth across the sand.

On the other side of him, the non-retching side, Caden moaned. He tried to sit up, but quickly fell back, his light-fingered hands pressing against his forehead. "Uggggh, this is the worst!" Caden said, trying to laugh. "Worse than any hangover, worse than no coffee for days. Jeff. Are you there?"

Jeff hmmed. "Worse than a hangover? You're a lightweight."

Caden laughed before moaning again. "We're alive, I guess that's a plus. What the fuck happened?"

"Jax knocked us out. Some kind of gas in the SU." Jeff felt a jab of anger, but after that, nothing. It was over.

"He played us pretty good then." Caden was sitting up now, a hand still on his forehead. They were both grey shadows to each other, but Jeff's eyes had had time to adjust and his head was finally clear. Caden's brown hair was silver and distinct in the starlight, his face grim. "Oh well," Caden continued in a cheerful voice. "The SUs are gone, we're without shelter or supplies on this ridge. It's horrendously cold," his grey body shuddered, "but hey, it's not the end of the world."

They sat next to each other, shivering, as the sky lightened to dark blue, then grey.

"We should go," Jeff said as he stumbled to standing and shook some of the cold from his body.

"Wait." Caden followed suit, stretching his arms above his head. He cracked his knuckles, seriously. "I want to check something first." Jeff hung back as Caden's silver-rimmed shadow strode to the drop off. Before Caden got to the edge, he stopped. "Jeff."

Jeff's knees ached with cold. His arms felt strange, as if they had been removed and then been replaced slightly off. The grey sky was running pink and orange, pastels seeping up, overtaking the last shred of night. He reached Caden then, and saw what he did. Hundreds of feet below the ridge, covering everything right up to the glowing horizon, was an ocean. The swishing he'd heard all night wasn't the wind. It was the sound of distant waves, swells breaking against the rocks sticking up like massive cones and spikes from the water, like towers, like skyscrapers, small as if seen from an airplane.

There was no sign of Jax or the SUs. No colony down there: only water stretching for ages and eons, diminished but still present in their empty world.

Neither of them said anything. The sun broke through the horizon, and light scattered over the waves like shards of glass. They walked closer to the edge, holding hands. They peered over until they found the bottom. There was no going on from here. Only back.

"It's not the end of the world," Caden smiled over at Jeff, "but it's pretty damn close."

They were stranded, on the ridge. No supplies, no idea of where they were. The SUs were gone. His bike and his covered trailer were gone. But Jeff wasn't afraid of it, the loss. Caden's presence was a warm hand interlaced with his. The shattered waves whispered up at them. The moment crystalized in Jeff's mind and in his body, a visceral memory of sadness and awe.

It was something he would remember for a very long time.

Brittni Brinn

Acknowledgements

I'm deeply indebted to all of my first readers—Chelsea Carey, Peter Brinn, Jean Brinn, Janine Marley, Lydia Friesen, Amilcar John Nogueira, Ben Van Dongen, and Christian Laforet.

Thanks to the following writers, artists, and creative communities, for everything from event invites to kind words—Windsor Zine Fair, The Windsor Small Press Book Fair, The Green Bean Cafe, Lowest Fi, Juniper Books, Kate Hargreaves, Cael Dobson, Gwen Aube, Elly Blake, Justine Alley Dowsett, Robert Dowsett, Sharon Ledwith, Jasper Appler, Hanan Hazime, Cindy Chen, Shawna Diane Partridge, Alexander Zelenyj, Elizabeth J. M. Walker, Sara Rolfes, Dawn Supina, Zachary Supina, Nicole Companyitsev, Sarah Kivell, Owen Swain, Vanessa Shields, Linda Collard, Joey Ouellette, and Michelle Heumann.

Also to everyone who read, reviewed, and supported my first book, *The Patch Project*. You wanted the story to continue and that was all the motivation I needed.

Amilcar John Nogueira edited this book, and I am so happy that they did. Characters now smile a lot less and the story is better for it.

Extra special thanks to Adventure Worlds Press. It is because of your efforts and constant encouragement that this book is in print. Looking forward to future writing sessions and rave book launches!

To my family, who are there for me in their own ways, always. Especially my parents for giving copies of my books to people and being all proud and parent-y about it.

And to Peter. For your sincere, exuberant, and at times hilarious support of what I do and who I am, I cannot say thank you enough.

Photo by Sarah Kivell

Brittni Brinn writes (mostly) post-apocalyptic fiction. She has a M.A. in Creative Writing, Language and Literature from the University of Windsor. Her interests include rocks kicked up by the ocean, books from friends, and comfortable sweaters. She currently lives in Windsor, Ontario along with her husband and two cats. You can read more about her work at: **brittnibrinn.com**.

AdventureWorldsPress.com

9 780994 980373